Axe River Bc

Short Story Prize Antho

Copyright © 2024 by Axe River Books CiC

All rights reserved. No part of this publication may be reproduced, distributed, or transmitted in any form or by any means, including photocopying, recording, or other electronic or mechanical methods, without the prior written permission of the publisher, except in the case of brief quotations embodied in critical reviews and certain other non-commercial uses permitted by copyright law.

Publisher: Axe River Books CiC
Axbridge, Somerset, United Kingdom
www.axeriverbooks.com

The stories contained in this anthology remain the intellectual property of their respective authors. The authors have granted Axe River Books CiC the non-exclusive right to publish their work in this anthology. All other rights revert to the authors upon publication.

ISBN: 9798327203952

Contents

Introduction   1

1.	Ripe Apricots, Boiling Oil	6
2.	Once for Yes	16
3.	Echoes	19
4.	The Curse	29
5.	Wanting to be John Wayne	34
6.	Seven Vials to Test the Limits of Sisterly Love	41
7.	Angle Eyes	50
8.	The King's Shilling	57
9.	The Lavender Witches	63
10.	Juggler	74
11.	The Real Fake News	83
12.	Happy New Year	93
13.	Cinderella (The True Story as Recounted by our Royal Correspondent)	102
14.	The Theory of Nothing	108
15.	A Day in the Life of the Seasons	117

INTRODUCTION

Axe River Books invited writers with unique stories to tell to submit fiction of up to 3,000 words on the Axe River Books website. There was no fee for entry and a £250 prize for the winning story. The winners were judged by Wrington-based novelist **MJ Greenwood**. Alongside the winning places one to five, we choose a further ten of the best stories to publish in the Axe River Prize Anthology, which you have in your hands.

Axe River Books is run by book lovers based in Somerset and takes its name from the Axe River that surfaces in the Wookey Hole Caves before flowing west along the feet of the Mendip Hills towards Brean Down and Weston Bay. Our priority is to find writers with original talent over commercial potential, and therefore, we have an open submissions policy, meaning writers do not need an agent to submit manuscripts.

We want a multidisciplinary output and will consider fiction, poetry, narrative nonfiction, and original creative projects for publication. The team behind the brand includes **Joe Williams**, full-time comms master, part-time theatre and music critic; **Emily Goodman**, short story writer and marketing strategist; and **Andy Corp**, media producer, photographer, and musician.

"Our goal in our first year is to find sincerely good writers, and we thought a short story contest would be a fantastic way to directly understand and tap into the talent pool in the West Country. We were thrilled to see so many submissions and reading all the entries was a joy. It was hard to whittle down our favourites, but there were some clear winners. Thanks so much to everyone who got involved by sending in work, reading or helping us organise, but especially to our judge, Mel, who put in some serious reading hours and gave us very heartfelt responses to each individual text." – Axe River Books Co-Founder, Emily Goodman.

"Seeing this book come to life after months of hard work has been an exciting journey. We owe a huge thanks to all our authors, our judge, and Gemma Trickey for her incredible support in making this dream a reality. This anthology is just the beginning–we look forward to continuing our mission of publishing great writing from the region." – Axe River Books Co-Founder, Joe Williams.

Congratulations to our winners. We hope you enjoy reading all the fabulous short stories as much as we did.

First: **Ripe Apricots and Boiling Oil, Clare Reddaway**

Second: **Once For Yes, Amanda Wynne**

Third: **Echoes, Mark Chivers**

Fourth: **The Curse, Jude Painter**

Fifth: **Wanting to be John Wayne, Paul Barnett**

OUR WINNER

Clare Reddaway is a versatile writer based in Bath, known for her plays, short stories, and articles. Her debut novel was published in March 2024, marking her exploration into longer prose fiction. Clare's deep passion for storytelling is evident in her performances at various events and festivals across southern England, and her plays, celebrated for their strong narratives and innovative theatricality, have been performed nationwide.

Her short stories have garnered critical acclaim, with long listings and short listings in prestigious competitions such as the BBC National Short Story Award and the Bridport Prize. Clare's works have been published in various anthologies and magazines and have been broadcast on local radio and recorded for podcasts. With an MA in Creative Writing from Bath Spa University and a background in script editing and drama development at the BBC and Granada Television, Clare continues to enchant audiences with her performances and site-specific writing.

"I believe that stories are the bedrock of being human, and I find creating, tangling and untangling them a source of constant fascination." – Clare Reddaway.

OUR JUDGE

Melanie Greenwood writes under the name MJ Greenwood on the kitchen table in her 400-year-old cottage in the heart of Wrington village, near Somerset's Mendip Hills. She is an author, a former journalist and amateur gardener.

Her debut novel, The Blue Hour, published by Bad Press Ink in 2021, has been described as "the literary equivalent of a strong gin and tonic on a warm summer's evening: refreshing, invigorating and inspiring…a stunningly good debut," by novelist Louise Douglas and has an average of 4.5 out of 5 stars on Amazon.

"Short stories are the very essence of telling tales that linger in your thoughts for far longer than the reading takes. I love that unique feeling when I'm plunged into another life, time or world, as if you're breathing the same air as the characters. It's one of the most difficult genres to get right, to make sure what you say is succinct and leaves its mark on the reader's mind, heart and soul." – MJ Greenwood.

OUR EDITOR

Emily Goodman (emilykaygoodman.com) has had short stories published in anthologies and online. She was shortlisted for the Wells Short Story Prize and longlisted for The Bristol Prize. She has an MA in Creative Writing from Bath Spa and has worked as a freelance marketer and writer for the last decade, working collaboratively with artists and businesses to bring stories to life.

"Editing this anthology was all about preserving the authentic voice and unique perspective each writer brought to their story. My aim was not to alter the narratives themselves (these stories needed no reworking) but to unify them through careful attention to style and clarity. I collaborated with each author to refine language where needed and ensure that each piece shone within the anthology's larger framework. Every story remains true to its original submission; no elements were reimagined or reshaped, allowing this collection to stand as a genuine reflection of each writer's vision." – Emily Goodman

A huge thanks to Andy Corp and Joe Williams who read through all the blind submissions and collaborated with our judge to create the final list of stories for inclusion. And to Joe Williams and Dr Jenny McNamara, proofreaders of the pre-sale copies.

1. Ripe Apricots, Boiling Oil

Clare Reddaway

I watch the sun set over the sea. I like to catch the moment when the tips of the waves are crested with gold, and I think of a faraway sea where the sun caresses the waves in the selfsame way. I look out now over this foreign ocean, which for a second reminds me of home, and I remember. The velvet of a ripe apricot soft beneath my thumb, the skin so easy to bruise and tear. The scent of attar of roses in a bedroom as the dusk rolls in. If I had the skill of a miniaturist, I would scratch an image on flattened bone: a rose, an apricot, a cresting wave. I would take the thinnest brush and colour with cochineal and indigo and frost the tips with gold. If I were a poet, I would capture the essence of the moment when the hand that lies on my arm is as warm as an apricot plucked in the midday heat and as full of promise as a sun that floods the world with gold. But I am neither miniaturist nor poet, and as I watch the waves, I hear Gav.

'Ham,' he calls. 'Break's over.'

And even though my cigarette is only half smoked, I wet my fingers, I pinch it out, and I turn, and I smile, and I hunch my shoulders and I say 'I am sorry, Gav, here, I am back.' I glance at the waves. The sun has gone. They are only grey.

The temperature of the oil must be just right. There is a way of telling. You must watch the bubbles in the corner of the vat. If the bubbles are too big, the fish will burn and must be thrown out. If they are too small, the fish will soak up all the oil and flop and sag. Then the fish is not thrown away but served to the tourists who will never return to the stall as they are only visiting the promenade for a day trip. When the oil is the perfect temperature, the fish will sizzle, and the batter will be crisp, and the fish cooked to perfection. This, Gav tells me, is the skill. This is what he will teach me: to anticipate and control the perfect temperature. His father taught him, and Gav will teach his son, although his son is only 18 months old. Gav is proud of his skill, I can see, and I admire it. But I hate the oil. I hate the speed with which it changes, the currents that I see swirling in its filthy depths. I hate the way it ferments, the way it spits, the clustering of bubbles around the fish as it is plunged in, as though the oil wants to consume the fish… Sometimes, I let a drop of oil fall onto the flesh of my arm and onto the pale underside near my wrist as an experiment. Boiling oil reaches a much higher temperature than boiling water.

The pain is excruciating. I aim to count to fifteen before wiping the oil away and running cold water over my arm. Yesterday, I got to 9. The flesh of my arm is puckered red. Gav sees the blisters, and he is surprised. He wonders how I had got so many burns. His, he says, are mainly on his forearms. He shows me, shrugging at his battle scars. I nod. Tomorrow, I will wear long sleeves.

The Civil War was a time of great upheaval in England. It began in 1642, and the winner was parliamentarian Oliver Cromwell. His reign heralded a period of extreme religious fundamentalism. He banned books. Theatres. Dancing. He died in…he died in…I have forgotten…

Tonight, I will send another postcard to my wife. I always choose a bland picture, a bright seaside scene with sand and blue water and children playing on a beach. Once, there were donkeys with children riding on them. I thought that might make my wife laugh. I hope it did. Maybe only a smile. A twitch of her lips, a glimpse of her teeth, her pink tongue. This time, the image shows the promenade, and it is possible to see the striped awnings of the stalls with their blackboard menus 'Fish and Chips'. I am sending her a picture of my workplace. I am sending her a message. Come! Find me! I do not know if she is suffering because of what I did. I do not know if she is still alive. I know I put her in danger with my postcards even though I leave them blank. I do not sign them. I do not send a message. The cards could be from anyone. I cannot bear to cut this last thin, wavering thread back to my heart. But the authorities will know they are from me. They could trace me. I have been reckless. The postcards have Weston-Super-Mare in tiny black letters on the left-hand side. But they will not follow me here to the edge of England, to this remote spike of land jutting into the sea. They will not bother. They have broken me. They have won.

I show Gav a picture of my wife. The photograph is creased, of course, worn, but I can see her face…and his face. I can see the curve of her cheek, her warm skin, her fingers.

'She's well gorgeous', says Gav. 'Is that your daughter?'

'My son,' I say, and I press my burnt arm to my side to feel the pain. My son. What lessons is he learning about his father now?

King John signed the Magna Carta in 1215 at Runnymede, enshrining liberties that would influence the world. I wanted to visit Runnymede to stand on the island where this landmark of freedom was drawn up. I asked Gav. He's never heard of Runnymede.

I was popular with my students. I was one of the favoured tutors, a teacher who could go into a classroom and still the clamour with a smile. All eyes would turn, shining, to me. The school admired me. As they should; I had a first from Tehran University, a postgraduate degree. No other teachers had such a prestigious background. I could have stayed in Tehran, continued my research, and taken up a post at the university. I could have opted to study abroad. America, even, if I was lucky. But I chose to return to my hometown. It is my passion – to educate to mould young minds. I believe that the future of a country lies behind the desks in its schoolrooms. I was lucky – I managed to get a job at one of the best academies in the city. I taught all levels, all senior years. I worked hard, long hours. I would pour over the students' essays, making suggestions adding comments. My colleagues would laugh – 'Just give them a B+' they would say, 'Don't you have a home to go to?' But I wanted to help my students attain the success I knew they were capable of. I wanted to open their minds to knowledge. And I certainly did have a home to go to. In the evenings, I would walk through the gate into the yard, and my wife would be waiting for me, and we would sit beneath the pomegranate tree and sip tea and eat walnuts and talk about our day and our future and our son.

'Another bag of chips when you're ready.'

She is leaning on the counter, her finger rootling in the paper corners of the first bag she bought. She takes her finger out of the bag. It is covered in salt. Slowly, slowly, she licks the salt off her finger as she looks at me. Her eyes are pale and lined with kohl. Her eyelashes are thick with black and stuck together. The grease from the chips has made her lips slick, and there is a smear of oil on her chin. I cannot take my eyes away from her finger.

'Cheeky,' she says. 'When you're ready, chuck. With the chips.'

Gav is on a break. He has gone to his caravan to have his tea. He will not be back for an hour. I am in charge. I stare at her finger. Her eyes are on me, knowing me, stripping me. Who are these women who look at me like they can see me naked and know my desires?

I scoop a portion of chips into a bag. I shake on vinegar. I shake on salt. I hand her the bag.

'How much?' she says.

I can't help myself. 'No money,' I say. And I raise my eyebrows and jerk my head to the door behind me. She smiles. I pull down the shutter. And she is there in the shack, her lips on mine, her hands on my body, she is on her knees, my back is against the vat of oil, and as I cum I think I should put my whole hand, my whole body into the boiling oil – but I am a coward, and I don't.

'What time you off then?' she says.

'Midnight,' I say.

Midnight. My wife was in labour for two days before my son was born. Two minutes after midnight. She told me she forgot the pain once she held him in her arms, but I have not forgotten. When I was seven, a dog was run over by a car in the street outside my house. The screams my wife made when she was giving birth were like the screams of that dog as he lay dying. And then there was our son, Fahim. Long and thin and wet with blood and mucus, a streak of black hair on his head, his mouth gaping like a hungry chick and the love that I felt flooded over me like nothing I had ever experienced before.

The 'Declaration of the Rights of Man' was signed during the French Revolution. It is a foundation stone of free speech, but it is soaked in the blood of the guillotine. It was written by... The name is...His name...Once, I would not have had to pause to think. Now... How could

I stand in front of a room of students? I have lost my confidence. I could not do it. I do not dare.

When Gav locked the shed up at midnight, she was sitting on the sea wall waiting for me.

'Whoa,' said Gav, and he nudged me with a smile on his face. He is not an unkind man. 'Go on then,' he said, 'I'll finish up here,' and I went to her. We walked to the beach and lay down under the stars.

Afterwards, she said, 'Shall we go back to yours?' but I live in the hostel. The people there are wild and drunk, and I find needles in the bathroom every morning. I hate it so much sometimes I choose to lie on the beach and listen to the waves all night. My body aches in the morning, and I can feel my joints. I have sucked the damp from the air inside myself. But she cannot come to the hostel.

'I'll be off then,' she says. 'Don't fancy kipping on the beach.'

'What's your name?' I ask.

'Jazz. Short for Jasmine. See ya'.' Jasmine. Yasmina.

I think of dark almond eyes, and as I stare at the stars, I weep.

I was pleased when the head of department assigned me the Second World War in Europe. I have a particular interest in the period, and it was my special subject for my degree. My students were engaged. They have seen films – some banned, of course – on the internet. It is one of the more accessible areas of history for the young. I was teaching the students about Hitler and the Final Solution. They had all heard President Ahmadinejad on the television. They knew his views. I was telling them about Mein Kampf. We read an extract in class. I discussed it with them – what did Hitler want to do to the Jews?

'Exterminate them!' shouted Samen. 'Good riddance!'

Free speech means allowing words to be uttered even if we disagree with them. To give them air leaches the poison from them, I believe. We discussed how Hitler carried out his plan.

'The Holocaust is a myth,' shouted Samen. 'The president has told us so.' I showed them pictures of the liberation of Belsen. The bodies of the starving.

'It is a construct of Western imperialism, a plot cooked up by the Jews to boost support for the state of Israel,' said Samen, but he was no longer shouting. I read them extracts from Primo Levi. I showed them pictures of Auschwitz, of the piles of suitcases, of the room full of spectacles. Samen was silent. Yeeessss!!

The euphoria that flooded my body was similar to the night my son was born. I was triumphant. I could change minds. I could change hearts. I could ensure that the voice of history sang out in all its truth and majesty! We would learn the lessons history can teach us. We would avoid the mistakes of the past. This generation would make up their own minds! I had started with one student, Samen, but I could speak to the whole of Iran! Oh, if only I had stopped there. If only I had enjoyed my success and then turned to my son and pushed his toy train across the yard so that he squealed with delight. But I didn't.

There is no one in this town who speaks my language. There is no one who knows anything about my country. Gav says that he knows it's religious. And hot. He says he wishes it was as hot here. Then he'd open an ice cream shack and sell ice creams instead of burning himself once a week at a vat of boiling oil. Even the food around me is alien. I can cook in the hostel where I live, and sometimes I take a fish that is left over, and I grill it with a squeeze of lemon. I eat it with a salad of cucumber, yoghurt, and salt, and I think about how much I have sacrificed, and I wonder whether I was right.

Socrates drank hemlock rather than be silent. Galileo insisted to the Inquisition that the earth does revolve around the sun. And I...I was warned that the secret police had read my article. I knew that they would come for me.

'Why did you write it? Did you care nothing for us?' Those are the words of my wife, of my Yasmina. She was sobbing so hard I could barely hear them. They are burnt into my memory, and daily, I ask myself, why did I write it? Was I right to make that choice? I knew it was dangerous, I knew the words were forbidden, I knew that to say the Holocaust happened made me an agent of our enemy, Israel, but I knew too that it was true and that to say nothing would be wrong. But did it have to be me?

The sacrifice was great. To pack my belongings into a suitcase. To take a favourite photograph of Yasmina and our son Fahim. To hold her close and to squeeze her body into mine so that I would feel the imprint forever. To open the gate in the yard and to slip out for the last time, at dead of night, before they came and dragged me out in front of my family and threw me into jail. Before they beat me, tore out my fingernails, and thrust my hands into burning oil. Before they took me, I slid away. I was helped, of course. Friends met me, fed me, gave me a bed, then drove me, passed me from one to another, shook my hand and clasped my shoulder as I walked over the border to Turkey and then on across Europe, to Britain, to England, to the home of free speech and then on until I washed up here.

If I had the skill of a miniaturist, I would paint Yasmina's face on a piece of flattened bone, and I would hold it next to my heart. If I were a poet, I would capture the bloom of her skin, the timbre of her voice, the quickening in my blood when I heard her footstep. But I am neither. I am a history teacher. I am a refugee. I am a deputy fish and chip cook. This is who I am. And now, this is who I will be. Forever.

2. Once For Yes

Amanda Wynne

'Knock once for yes, twice for no.' Fiona repeated.
She tightened her grip on her two neighbours' hands, took a deep breath and bowed her head. The gold sequins sewn to the edge of her scarf tickled her forehead.
        'Knock once for…'
        A frantic series of seven raps sounded from the cabinet behind her.

Mrs Hardie, Mrs Oakley and Mrs Charlton bounded up out of their chairs in alarm.

'Please, please…' Still seated, Fiona beckoned them to sit back down.

Ashen-faced and wide-eyed, one by one, they complied.

To Fiona's right, Mrs Hardie wore a mismatched assortment of vintage gold rings. The tweed blazer she wore over her cardigan squeezed her arm tight, restricting her movement. It pinched at her bicep as she raised her arm up to take Fiona's hand.

Opposite Fiona, the stern-faced Mrs Oakley wore a large floral print kaftan over bangled arms. To Fiona's left sat Mrs Charlton, her with a stiff khaki green woollen skirt and jacket, with pearls around her neck.

Fiona guessed they were all in their late sixties. Mrs Oakley and Mrs Charlton were there for support. Mrs Hardie had sought Fiona's services to discuss a matter of great import with her late husband.

Fiona took a deep breath.

'Mr Hardie, is the jewellery box in the loft of your house?' She said. 'Knock once for yes, twice for no.'

This time, there were thirteen answering knocks, rapid as machine gun fire.

The ladies stayed in their seats, white-knuckling their held hands.

'What does that mean, Mr Hardie?' Said Fiona, eyes closed, chin down.

[It means I'm not telling that woman a damn thing.]

Fiona sighed through her nose.

'What does THAT mean, Mr Hardie?' She said.

[It means she can go to hell.]

More loud raps on the cabinet door.

Beside her, Mrs Hardie squeaked. Fiona squeezed her hand tighter.

'Mr Hardie is speaking to me.' Said Fiona, swaying her head, catching the candlelight in the scarf's sequins.

'Oh!' Mrs Hardie bumped the table with her belly. 'What's he saying about the jewellery box?'

[You're not having it.]

'He's thinking.' Fiona smiled placidly.

[She's not having it!]

'Dale, darling. You know I miss you so much.' Mrs Hardie cooed. 'Where did you put the box?'

[Up my backside.]

Fiona bit her lip.

'He…I'm sorry, Mrs Hardie, he says he doesn't remember.'

Mrs Hardie's face fell.

'Really?'

Fiona nodded.

[Tell her I don't want her to have it.]

'He says he's sorry he can't help you.'

More loud knocks on the cabinet made them all jump.

'He's really frustrated he can't be more helpful.' Fiona grimaced apologetically. 'Is there anything else you'd like to ask him about?'

Mrs Hardie shook her head. A tear traced its way down her powdered cheek.

[I never loved you.]

'He says he loves you very much.'

There was a single large thwack to the side of the cabinet, nearly splitting the wood.

'Once for yes.' Fiona smiled sweetly.

Only she heard the howl, but they all saw the candles blow out as something unseen exited the room in disgust. Around her, the women screamed.

Fiona moved to the window and pulled the heavy curtains back, slowly flooding the room with sunlight and rainbows cast from the row of crystals hanging on chains from the windowpane.

Her guests blinked in the light.

'I think that concludes our session, ladies.' Said Fiona. 'Mrs Hardie, will that be cash or credit?'

3. Echoes

Mark Chivers

To those who were unfamiliar with the wetlands, the deep reverberations of the bittern's call might have been mistaken for the sound of a horn. But Nara was of the Lake People, and through her youth, she was already attuned to the noises of the unseen creatures that lived in the meandering mire. Nara was determined to catch a bittern for the spit and had been practising with her sling. The leather strap hung limp from her clenched fist while her other hand rested on the pouch of baked clay shots at her belt.

Listening for the bird, Nara continued moving away from the village through the tufts of sedge and skirted the edge of the woods. Her eyes were trained on the wall of reeds to her right as she stepped onto one of the walkways across a bog.

Grandmother had told her that much longer wooden trackways had linked the islands of the wetlands many generations ago. But the sea had crept into the valley, inundating the land. Canoes were the easiest way to traverse this habitat. Nara's father and older brother were out there in one today, slipping along the scrub and reed-lined avenues with their fishing nets and bow.

Nara paused on the oak planks of the trackway above the still, black water. The two-tone boom of the bittern was sounding again, nearer this time. She lifted the sling slightly, sliding her fingers into the pouch to retrieve a shot. The bird called again. It seemed to be further along the track now. She continued walking, placing her feet carefully.

Looming over the alder, birch, and willow trees ahead was the bulbous form of Ynys Wydryn. The hill was a dark blue smudge against the cloud-laden horizon, a proud promontory in an otherwise flat landscape of swamp and fenland. Nara moved further towards the treeline. She saw movement at the edge of a nearby pool. Again, the call came, and Nara felt the bass and the excitement in her chest as she spotted the mottled brown bird perching on a bundle of thick stalks. With each note, its feathered throat engorged and then deflated.

Hunched low behind a bush, Nara placed a shot into her sling and began to spin it. The bittern glanced up askance, and for a moment, she thought that it had seen her. But the bird resumed its call. Nara rose to fling her shot. There was a sudden splash behind her, which caused a trio of ducks to burst from cover. Startled, Nara sent her shot wide as the bittern hauled itself into flight, sailing away over the reeds.

"Nara!"

She wheeled around and saw her younger brother Uric, one leg submerged in the mire, his hands grasping at the trailing curtain of a small, crooked willow.

"Help, Nara!"

"Uric! Why are you here? I told you to wait in the village."
Tucking the sling into her belt and wrapping an arm around the tree, Nara leaned to grasp Uric's wrist. She hauled him back onto firm ground. His boots, leg bindings, and trousers were sodden and plastered in mud.

"Want to hunt with you," said Uric.

"You are not yet old enough."

"Or slay a wyrm!"

"Well, you are certainly too young to be slaying," said Nara with a smile.

Uric tried to scrape some of the mud from his leg but only made his hands dirtier. He shivered slightly, looked about the ground, and picked up his wooden toy axe.

"Let us return to the village," said Nara. She unfastened the heavy bronze pin at her neck and slung her flax-and-maroon plaid cloak around her brother's shoulders. The hem of the outsize garment dragged along the damp earth as the boy walked beside his sister.

The thatched cones of the roundhouses emerged from among the scrub and scattered trees.

Faint wisps of smoke drifted from the peaks of the roofs. The children passed through one of the gaps in the palisade that bordered the village, between a pair of stakes topped with human skulls. Father had told Nara the tale of a battle from before her birth: these were the heads of Belgic raiders from the eastern lands, wards against enemies of the Lake People.

Nara and Uric strolled between the clusters of houses and animal pens along the path that led to their home near the open water on the far side. The village nestled on a river, the channels of which wound beyond the ridgeline to the north, out into the estuary valley of the Mynydd Hills. Trade from settlements up and down the river flowed through the village.

Leaning over a wattle fence, Nara scratched the hairy back of her favourite pig, who snorted in appreciation. Along the main path, which snaked through the village, the siblings passed racks of stretched animal skins, a group of women weaving baskets, and a man steaming strips of wood to fashion into boxes. Shouts and laughter from other children could be heard. The pathways were interspersed with clumps of thick grass, scattered with marsh marigolds and purple ragged robins in places, especially where older roundhouses had reached the end of their lives and crumpled in on themselves, reclaimed by the green earth.

As Nara and Uric approached their own home, they saw the neighbouring family building their new house. The walls were already defined by a circle of posts, broken by a large square porch, and densely interwoven with slimmer willow branches. This wattle stretched into a half dome where the roof began, but the thatching was yet to be added. Today, the whole household was arduously mixing clay, straw, and animal dung to daub the framework of the walls.

"What happened to you two?" asked their mother, who was returning from the riverside with a basket of washed clothes. Sedobel stood looking down at them, basket on her left hip, right hand on her other. Their mother wore a woollen dress similar in cut to Nara's, but instead of plain russet like her daughter's, Sedobel's was chequered in vivid blues.

"I went out of the village, and Uric followed me."

"I asked that you stay here and look after him, Nara."

"He was playing with the other children when I left. I only went because I heard a bittern. I thought I could catch it quickly."

"Uric is too young to wander beyond the village alone."

"I know, mother. I am sorry."

Sedobel sighed and tucked a long braid of auburn hair behind her ear.

"Take your brother inside and change his wet clothes."

"Yes, mother," said Nara, taking Uric's hand and leading him into their roundhouse, one of the smaller abodes. The children were embraced by the reassuring warmth and smoky air of their home: a single limewashed circular chamber in which they lived with their parents, older brother, and Grandmother Suli. Bundles of dry herbs, fish, and waterfowl hung from beams above. Their grandmother was sat tending the pot which simmered over the central hearth. Suli smiled at Nara and Uric, her lined face friendly amidst her loose locks of grey hair. Her voice was croaky when she spoke.

"It looks as if you have been adventuring little ones. I expect that you will be hungry."

Later that day, after the evening meal, Nara lay in her cot. The sleeping areas were divided by drapes, and she watched the silhouettes of her parents and older brother flicker across the material as the glow of the hearth subsided. Gently, the realm of sleep claimed Nara, though she did not recognise the transition.

She was at the meet that took place every summer on the shore of the great lake west of their village. Kith and traders had traversed the wetlands from long distances, from over the hills and from the faraway coast. They came to renew bonds, exchange, and barter. It was Nara's favourite time of the yearly cycle. So many people gathered in one place, and so much excitement in the activities and crafts being plied. There were a few roundhouses at this seasonal site, but the majority of people were gathered under tents and awnings, and the northern breeze from across the lake was held at bay by lines of willow windbreaks. A great feast was being prepared in cauldrons filled with smaller vessels, which bubbled on open hearths.

Nara ran from one place to another, holding Uric's hand. Her eyes feasted on beautiful necklaces of colourful glass and amber beads, cloak pins and brooches of intricate design, patterned fabrics in myriad colours, gleaming iron spears and swords, and masterfully wrought shields with decorative bronze bosses. Here, a group of men were gambling raucously over a game of dice. There, the betrothal of a young couple was sealed with the cheer of their gathered kin. All became a whirl of dancing, feasting, and merriment through the long summer day, and even when darkness finally settled over the meet, the fires obstinately flared their orange glow through the night.

It was a cold, grey day, the landscape shrouded in thick mist. Nara stood at the edge of the mire, between her mother and father. Their faces were reflected with crystal perfection on the surface of the water. Uric was no longer holding her hand. She glanced up at her parents in turn, but their eyes were fixed on a group of indistinct figures at the other side of the pool. When she opened her mouth to speak, her throat was silent. Neither her mother nor her father seemed to see Nara. She felt very small.

Across the water, three of the figures stepped forward. A bearded druid loomed in the middle, dressed in a white robe and bearing a carved oak staff. The other two people carried between them a corpse dressed in fine clothing. His limbs were bound, weighted with stones, and his pale hands grasped the haft of an axe tight to his chest.

This was the funeral of Nara's grandfather. But something wasn't right.

The druid spoke of Domnu, primordial goddess of the deep earth and sea depths, of how the deceased was being returned to her, and of how his body would be reclaimed and his spirit would pass into the Otherworld to be reborn. At a gesture from the druid, the corpse-bearers eased their burden into the dark water of the pool, allowing the body to slip from this world towards the next. The surface of the mire broke into ripples, shattering the faces of Nara and her parents.

Nara woke with a gasp.

"Uric! Uric, where are you?"

Someone was calling her brother's name. She flung the furs from her, stood, and dressed in a rush. Bleary-eyed from sleep and squinting in the bright morning light outside the roundhouse, Nara found her mother and older brother Nouant looking for Uric. Several other villagers were nearby, concern on their faces.

"Nara. You slept heavily. Nouant could not wake you," said her mother. "Uric was up with father this morning, but now he is missing."

"Father is readying the canoe. We will search along the river," said Nouant. He hurried down to the jetty, where several other men were climbing into canoes to join the search. Other villagers were heading out into the fenland, some carrying rope and staves.

Beginning to panic, the events of yesterday whirled through Nara's mind. She remembered Uric retrieving his little wooden axe.

"I think that I know where he is," said Nara, not waiting for her mother to reply before she hitched up the hem of her dress and sprinted across the village and into the wilderness. Hoping that Uric remembered the route as well as she did, Nara sped through the patchwork landscape, avoiding bog, skirting briar, and deftly crossing walkways as she wound her way towards the woods.

She could hear the others shouting Uric's name as they searched for him.

A short distance inside the treeline, in a swampy depression, a huge, gnarled willow tree stood alone. It was borne out of the morass of thick mud and moss on twisted roots like muscular limbs, and it leaned haphazardly over the firmer ground like a great rearing beast. This was Uric's 'wyrm': one of his favourite places that Nara had taken him to, and it was here that she found him.

Ava sipped some more tea from her flask, a broad smile on her face, though she stood alone. The morning eruption of tens of thousands of shimmering starlings had been exhilarating. Perhaps not as impressive as the murmurations near sundown could be; but the cloud of cacophonous birds bursting from the reeds and whirling overhead as they flew out to feed in the fields had been a thrilling start to the day.

With only a handful of other spectators this early in the morning, the display had possessed a special resonance.

It was still an hour or so until she was due on site, so Ava walked further along the track, rubbing her gloved hands to keep warm and occasionally lifting her binoculars at the sight or sound of waterfowl out in the reedbeds.

Eventually, Ava headed back to her car at the edge of the reserve and drove the short distance to the car park. Deep, lurid green drainage ditches lined the side of the road, which undulated dramatically with the soggy ground beneath. Eerie pockets of vapour drifted low to the frosty ground, swirling aside as the car passed through them.

Ava retrieved her toolbox from the boot, locked the vehicle with a press of a button, and strode across the gravel into the grounds of the visitor centre. A few other volunteers had begun to arrive, donning their work boots and warm coats. With smiles and greetings, they assembled in the yard between the Saxon hall, the Viking longboat, and the Romano-British villa. Before them was a circle of willow posts driven into the ground and bundles of thinner branches. The volunteers set to work on the wattle of the walls.

By lunchtime, they had woven all around the base of the roundhouse structure. After proudly admiring their handiwork, the volunteers strolled over to the Saxon hall to warm up and eat. Somewhere in the distance, over the chatter and sounds of eating, there came a distinct call.

"Do you hear that?" asked Ava through a mouthful of crisps.

If she had been sitting there two-thousand-two-hundred years earlier, Ava might have thought of hunting when she heard the boom of the bittern somewhere in the veil of mist that lay across the Levels. The Iron Age was long past and buried. This was the Plastic Age. But still, the bird's call sent a shiver down Ava's spine.

4. The Curse

Jude Painter

Things are generally fine in the kingdom at present. The common folk go about their business in their usual sulky fashion, and things at the palace just tick on as normal. My husband is, to all intents and purposes, the most royal commander and ruler, but everyone with any sense knows that most of the important decisions and proclamations originate with myself, his queen. However, I don't always get everything right, especially where our daughter is concerned. She is a teenager and has always been a very difficult child. There was something important I had to talk to her about before her birthday next week, so I took the unusual step of heeding advice from an 'expert'.

Years ago, all villages had an idiot or two who would stand in the marketplace on Wednesdays and shout nonsense. Everyone tended to just ignore them or hurl rotten vegetables at them, and it all worked very well and was quite a lot of fun. But now, all that has stopped. People no longer visit the market to hear the nonsense. It comes direct to their homes. There are hollow pipes which go into every home in the kingdom. Anyone can just shout whatever they like up or down them; everyone gets to hear it, whether they want to or not. Sometimes, the voices make strange claims about magical potions that can cure all manner of diseases. In the palace, our tube comes up in the dining room, where I usually just shove a cork into it. However, yesterday, I happened to hear some instructions for removing the warts from enchanted frogs. Useful, as I know for a fact that many handsome princes have had their lives blighted when, after their transformation, they still retained their unsightly green frog warts, something no princess would want to kiss more than once. But, to get back to the voice. It claimed to be from a relationship counsellor and promised to improve my interactions with both family and friends. It told me how to enhance my communication skills and empathy with teenagers, which I thought might be useful.

So today, I trailed up the hundred and seventy-nine steps to my daughter's tower (why do they always have to have their bedrooms in towers, I'd like to know?) to confront her. Needless to say, she was sleeping again. I sank to my knees in a welter of discarded clothes, platters of food remnants and dirty coffee vessels and tried to catch my breath.

I had learned from the person speaking up the hollow tube that one must not say 'I think we should have a talk' to teenagers as that immediately warns them and makes them stop listening.

"So," I began with a bright remark designed to capture her interest and show I was up to date with the latest trends, and also to encourage a meaningful response, "have you heard the latest lyre music?"

"No," she replied, sitting up and yawning."

"You used to love the lyre when you were a little girl," I said...Fondly, I hoped.

"Duh…!" she replied, rolling her eyes. "Everyone knows it's the sackbut now, lyres are soooo last century."

I pressed on, "Yesterday, I was thinking about the music at your christening. You know it was a lovely occasion. There was pink cake, and all the fairies came and gave you wonderful gifts."

She brightened at this, "What sort of wonderful gifts? Why haven't I seen the wonderful gifts? What have you done with them?

"The fairies said they gave you things like beauty, wealth and a lovely singing voice and, of course, your gorgeous golden hair." As I said this, I thought that, in reality, heredity and genetics had a lot to do with it. I have very nice hair myself. But that's the thing about fairies. They always want to take all the credit.

"Oh! My hair, I hate my hair. I wish I had beautiful hair like my friend. She has long waving hair, and she has these really strong extensions. It is so long that she lets it hang out of the window, and it's just amazing. Why can't I have some extensions?" She began glaring at herself in the mirror. "I'm so ugly. I hate myself."

I could tell she was trying to distract me or else fishing for compliments. However, I needed to explain to her about the curse from the bad fairy, who was just some disgruntled distant relation with issues we had forgotten to invite to the christening.

"No, darling, you are beautiful," I began. "People even call you Sleeping Beauty (and here I might have made a mistake). "Although you could try to be a bit more energetic, you don't get up before lunchtime."

As the person who called herself a life coach had warned me, I found I was in danger of losing my focus and starting to become irritated.

I tried a different tack. "You may have wondered why we don't have a team of eager seamstresses about the palace, mending things and making our curtains and loose covers or why we have to always make do with ready-made clothes?" I persisted. "You may have wondered why we never let you do embroidery like other princesses do...?"

"No, not at all. You never let me do what everyone else is doing. You're so mean!"

She paused and looked out of the window at the village pond where a joyful crowd had gathered to watch a witch being plunged into the water on a ducking stool. This seemed to cheer her up. She looked at me with a sudden bright smile. "I know what I want for my birthday."

"Yes," she said, clasping her hands together. "It's something all my friends have...a tattoo. Just a little one. I thought of a tiny pink dragon peeping out from my armpit. It would be really cute...Ooh, mummy, please!"

I gritted my teeth, knowing that the fateful occasion was just four days away, and I had still not managed to find the words to tell her that according to the curse after she was pricked on that day, she and the whole palace would fall asleep for one hundred years. I had taken as many precautions as possible all her life, keeping sharp things away, and now began to wonder if maybe I should just let the curse take its toll.

If you've got teenagers, you'll probably understand. I honestly didn't have the energy to argue anymore, and the idea of having a nice rest for a hundred years suddenly felt very appealing. So, I just found myself agreeing. I let her send a messenger to summon the tattooist and went off to find somewhere comfortable where I could have a nice lie down for a century or so.

5. Wanting to be John Wayne

Paul Barnett

When I was seven years of age, Maggie Farrell claimed me as her boyfriend. I didn't quite see it that way, but I didn't dare say otherwise. She'd tricked me into going into her uncle's pigeon coop and wouldn't let me out until the deal was done.

"Will you be my boyfriend now, Marty?" Maggie said, sat on the wall outside, swinging her legs, looking up from her book, The Fantastic Mr Fox. Maggie was forever reading when she wasn't concerning herself with my being her boyfriend.

"I will not," I said firmly, though those pigeons were starting to flap, and I was desperate to pee.

"Those pigeons," Maggie whispered through the wire mesh. "'Ave been known to peck a boy's eyes out."

Well, that was it. I started screaming the place down, running on the spot, and before I knew it, I was wet at both ends.

"Okay, okay. I'll be your boyfriend," I said with a heavy sob.

"Kiss me first, and then I'll let you out."

Outside of the family, that kiss through the wire cage of the pigeon coop had been my first. Maggie said it made me officially her boyfriend, and there was no getting out of it now. I wasn't sure what was expected of me in the role, but Maggie said that didn't matter as she'd explain things as we went along. Apparently, her coming to my house any time she pleased was all part of the arrangement.

Maggie lived opposite, and her mother was best friends with my mother, so it wasn't like I didn't see enough of her already. Her father was no longer on the scene, though I was under strict instructions never to mention that fact; but God knows the temptation to blurt was never far away.

Maggie was taller than most of us; slender, short auburn hair, with freckles across her nose like an Apache Indian's war paint, and like an Apache, she'd stand no messing off anyone, including from boys bigger than herself. I once heard her mother say to my mother, she's a will of her own, that one; and I sort of knew what she meant. All the same, I couldn't help finding the back of Maggie's neck pretty, with its soft downy flecks of hair catching in the sunlight, though I never breathed a word of that to anyone.

"You're not playing with your doll again, are you, Marty McBride?" Maggie said as she came marching through our back gate and sat right down on the grass next to me.

I kissed her on the cheek, which, apparently, was another thing expected of a boyfriend, and in a forced whisper, I said, "It's not a doll."

"Looks like a doll."

In the nine days of our being boyfriend girlfriend, we kept having this debate, and it was beginning to nettle me something rotten.

"Well, it's not."

"Barbie has a boyfriend called Ken, and he looks just like…"

"This is Action Man, alright?" I said, rolling my eyes. "Ken doesn't have grenades, rifles, and a tank. He doesn't have bazookas. And he certainly doesn't have a flamethrower."

"Yeah, but he's still a doll."

"He isn't."

Although Maggie dressed like a boy, she hated war games of any kind. At the time, I wondered if she just couldn't help being a girl in that way, but maybe it was us lads who were lagging behind.

My mother appeared at the back door drying a glass on a towel and said, "Oh good, you're here, Maggie. Would you like to stop for tea?"

I tried to silence her with the power of my mind, but it didn't work.

Maggie beamed a big smile, nodded, and said, "Yes, please, Mrs McBride."

That was us set for the rest of the afternoon: me playing in the dirt with my soldiers and Maggie alongside reading Treasure Island. Somehow, my war games were never the same, never as good with Maggie around. I felt awkward, what with Maggie covering her mouth and giggling whenever I provided the sound effects to my battles; the sounds of the explosions persh, persh or the machine guns ratattata. I didn't get why she hated war games so much when war was an obsession with us boys. We had it on TV screens every evening right after Jackanory. What was going on in Vietnam was our tea-time viewing.

Back then, no one thought to question if all that violence was good for us. It didn't really matter to us boys anyway; in our heads, we mashed up what we saw on the news with the John Wayne films we endlessly watched. You knew where you were in a John Wayne film; good guys beating bad guys, and John Wayne, of course, always being on the side of the good. We all wanted to be John Wayne. We aped his walk, his talk. Well, howdy, Pilgrim, my friends and I would say to one another in a long, slow drawl, but Maggie never saw the joke. I was starting to think I didn't want to be her boyfriend anymore, though I wasn't sure how to get out of it.

Later that evening, after Maggie had left, I went and squatted on the stairs, which was just about the best place to hear anything that was going on. My eldest sister (I had the misfortune of having three, all older) was talking to my mother about Maggie's dad. She said that he was getting married again and that his new wife was having a baby. I felt sure I was on the trail of some important finding, but then my mother stuck her head out the kitchen door and said, "I best not catch you earwigging on those stairs, Marty McBride."

I gingerly tip-toed back to my bed, where I tried to make sense of what I had heard and how best to use it to my advantage.

A few days later an action film called The Sands of Iwo Jima was on television with John Wayne and his men storming beaches against their Japanese enemies. My mates wanted to recreate the action scenes we'd seen at The Mount which was where we held all our pretend battles. In truth, it was just a muddy hill left over from the builders of our estate but in turn, it had been an island, a castle, a fort, and every war zone imaginable.

I'd just left my house and was on my way to call for Declan when Maggie shouted over, "Where're you going, Marty?"

I told her about the film, about Iwo Jima, the battles, about wanting to be John Wayne. I couldn't help sounding excited. Maggie looked at me evenly, shook her head and said, "Ah no, you can't be doing that, Marty."

I didn't understand and just looked at her blankly, my brain trying to catch up and make sense of the information.

Maggie said, "You have to stay here and help me train Freeman."

Freeman was Maggie's terrier, so called because her mother got him from the dog's home and didn't pay a penny for him.

"But I want to play war…"

"Well, you can't. You're my boyfriend, and you have to stay here. It's what boyfriends do."

That did it.

"But I don't want to be your boyfriend, Maggie," I stormed. "If anything, I hate being your boyfriend, Maggie and do you know what? Your dad hates being your dad too. He's off now to be dad to someone else. Did you not know that?"

The instance the words were out, I was certain I'd gone too far. Maggie snorted, clenched her fists, and narrowed her eyes and I thought I was in for the biggest walloping of my life. But then something incredible happened. A single solitary tear set sail down Maggie's cheek and over her sprinkling of freckles, and she turned away. I watched as she walked slowly back to her house, slamming her front door behind her. It should have felt like a victory or something, but instead, I just felt bad, and I didn't know why.

When Maggie stopped calling round, my mother took me aside and said, "What did you say to upset that girl?"

"I didn't," I pleaded, and then looked down at my feet.

Things soon got back to normal, and I went back to playing war games with my friends. Whenever I left my house, Maggie would be sat on her front lawn reading, with Freeman panting at her side his tongue lolling. She never looked over, never waved, and smiled like she used to. I didn't care; being a boyfriend was stupid anyway, I thought.

Then one evening, after a day of long, hard-fought battles on The Mount, I went home for Sheppard's pie. Vietnam was on the news again when suddenly an image appeared on our TV screen, right in our front room, of a young girl, about my age, or maybe a little older, running down the middle of the road without any clothes on. The announcer said that a bomb or something called napalm had been dropped nearby. The girl was sobbing, as were all the other children in the scene. The newsreel was as shocking to me as it was confusing; the announcer said that those responsible were on the side of the Americans, on the side of John Wayne and his men. John Wayne wouldn't go dropping bombs on small children, I told myself. It just didn't make any sense. That night, I slept badly.

The next morning, when my friends called for me on their way to The Mount, I realised I no longer had the stomach for war games, and they went on without me. When I looked over, I saw Maggie sat on her front lawn, reading. On an impulse, I went across to see her. When I approached, she looked up and stuck her tongue out then went back to reading her book. I sat down anyway, as I didn't have anything better to do. For a long time, we didn't speak. Maggie carried on reading, ignoring me. Her mum, however, gave me an encouraging smile through the living room window. I'm not sure why. It never occurred to me to say sorry to Maggie.

Finally, Maggie looked at me and, with an exaggerated sigh, said, "What do you want, Marty?"

It was a direct question for which I didn't have a readymade answer, so I blurted, "I could be your boyfriend again…if you want."

"Won't be that easy, Marty McBride," Maggie said, disappearing back behind the cover of her book, but the smile she took with her told me otherwise.

6. Seven Vials to Test the Limits of Sisterly Love

Sarah Evans

I sit and wait. Around me, people toy with their mobile phones or engage in stranger chit-chat. Can you believe the weather for June? Feet tap to the pounding rhythms that seep out from earplugs. The others all seem unconcerned. I inhale the eau-de-hospital blend of sweat and floor cleaner as my eyes skim the printed words of my magazine, fear rendering me incapable of absorbing their meaning.

I've always hated anything medical. My hand trembles as I lift my bottle of water to my desert-dry mouth. I breathe in to a slow count of four, exhale to eight, and doing so I lose the reflex, feel myself struggle for oxygen, on the edge of hyperventilation.

Stop it! I tell myself, Stop being so ridiculous. Having blood taken is the most routine procedure in the world. Blood that will then be tested in a vast variety of ways, the first stage in a process. I am here not for myself but for my sister.

Then I remember back…

To the time my sister blamed me for our mother's severed necklace, though she was the one who'd taken a pair of scissors to the linking thread, just experimenting, not expecting, not really, the glinting beads to roll off every which way into darkened corners. I failed to properly deny her accusation, and she watched – smugness playing on her lips – as I endured Mum's crossness and was sent up to bed with no tea.

A voice calls out, "Simone Hinds?"

My turn. The simmering tension has failed to prepare me for the boiling over into panic. I could continue sitting here, disowning my name, waiting for the phlebotomist to move on to the next person on her list before quietly slipping away.

Instead, my weak-as-water legs lift me to standing. I feel like a toddler taking first uncertain steps as I walk towards the woman who sports her smile of professional reassurance. I do not smile back.

I follow her to a small cubicle, one of a whole long line-up, and she pulls a curtain across. Through it, I hear the murmur of distraction tactic chatter all around. The white-coated woman with a permanent smile has a badge. Elaine. This happens to be my sister's name, and the coincidence is disconcerting.

I sit on a luminously green chair while Elaine studies her printed page. I wonder how much this tells her, whether she can figure out my purpose in coming here and what her opinion might be. Opinions are not part of her job. She pulls a wry face.

"I'm going to need quite a few samples, I'm afraid."

I swallow sand. "How many?"

"Seven," is the reply, followed by, "Are you alright there?"

I smile feebly. I feel sick and muzzy. Not the sort of muzzy-ness that means I am imminently about to pass out, but the sort which could build and tip over into that. I fainted a few years ago when a phlebotomist screwed things up, prodding and poking and puncturing right through a vein. I want to ask this woman if she's competent. Not a question which would produce a sensible answer. More likely to piss her off or make her nervous. Not that she looks the nervous type.

"I hate this," I say, stating the bleeding obvious. And if I'm this crap at giving blood, then very clearly, I could never in a million years go through with the whole shebang, begging the question, why I'm even here?

My sister's type II diabetes has led to renal failure and dialysis three times a week. She is hoping to find a donor for a replacement kidney. Waiting lists for dead donors extend several years and deliver less good outcomes than live ones. Live donor generally means a blood relative because who in their right mind would give away part of their body to someone unless they were close?

Sisterhood does not necessarily imply closeness.

I remember...

My first day at school and my sister called me a worm in front of her friends. The nickname became contagious, and soon, all her classmates, mine, and the whole bloody school, nobody called me anything else.

The white-coated woman keeps on smiling. She must have seen it all, of course. There must be those even more pathetic than me, hard though this is to imagine.

"It shouldn't take long," she says. "Any preference as to which arm?" As if I am likely to have a favourite arm for bloodletting. I hold out my left. She examines it, her latex-enclosed fingers prodding at my elbow's inner crease. I gaze at the papery skin, the blue-maggot bulge of veins, and disquiet shivers through; instinctively, I recoil from all that happens beneath the surface, all the complex, messy inner workings. My mind is curiously resistant to picturing the functioning of the body that fuels it. As a healthy adult, this is rarely an issue.

Elaine-the-phlebotomist dabs alcohol on my skin, wraps a tourniquet loosely above my elbow and slowly, the band is tightened. The initial request came via my mother, who posed it in a way that seemed so eminently reasonable. A simple blood test just so we'd know one way or the other.

"No point thinking too far ahead at this stage," she said. Her own health has proved insufficiently robust to allow for a major operation, letting her conveniently off the hook.

"D'you have any holiday plans?" Elaine asks as she prepares the needle and vial, a blatant attempt to sidetrack my mind away from this unpalatable present. I will not be able to plan any sort of holiday if I take this thing forward.

"No," I say. Saying no is not difficult. Surely. Yes, is far too vast a thing to ask. Elaine-my-sister must see that. I picture how it will go. How each of the smaller asks will be difficult to refuse? If we arrive at that point at which all tests have delivered positive results, a final refusal will feel appallingly hard.

I remember...

The time my sister put a caterpillar down my back in church, though she knew I had a horror of anything creepy-crawly. Elaine gazed up to the heavens as her voice rang out, pure and sweet with some hymn, while I wriggled and squirmed, earning a sharp slap from my mother.

"Just a small prick," Elaine says, the way they always do. No puncture of skin and vein ever feels entirely trivial; it always hurts. I think of the time I underwent a general anaesthetic, the sheer terror at being told to count to ten, the knowledge that events had now moved beyond my control, and I was powerless to fight the drift into unconsciousness that would leave my body a slab of meat on a trolley, at the mercy of doctors and their instruments. I woke in a heartbeat, feeling sick and disorientated, with a thirst no gulping of water seemed to quench. And if a simple test felt so hard, how much worse for a major operation, one to remove a vital organ, leaving a permanent scarred reminder of my increased vulnerability? What if I need my second kidney? After all, isn't that why evolution has given us two?

Stop it! I instruct my overactive mind. Stop wandering off in unhelpful directions.

My mind remains immune to its own commands. It wanders back, remembering...

My sister told me ghost stories late at night in the dark, drawing me in with a silly, giggly spookiness, then ramping the fear up, taking me down ever darker pathways of imagination and leaving me with nightmares which, night after night, grew more terrifying. Mum told her to stop, but she didn't, forcing me instead into secrecy by detailing the gory punishments that awaited telltale tits.

"There," Elaine says. "One down, six to go."

Seven samples for multiple tests. There are two ways of being dealt a get-out-of-jail-free card. First is the question of tissue compatibility, and given how different my sister and I are, surely, it's not unreasonable to hope that my body part would be sod-all use to her anyway. The second is the finding of potential ill-health in me, a previously unknown heart defect, for example, or less than perfectly healthy kidneys.

I wonder how much of the second would be worth it to clear me from obligation?

Not that I am under any obligation. Elaine's doctor kept emphasising that this had to be my own freely arrived at decision, that I can, of course, back out at any point. It is hardly my responsibility that my sister's poor choices led to her developing a lifestyle disease which resulted in kidney failure. I do not owe her one of my carefully looked-after organs.

I keep on remembering back...

How she stole attention at every family event, always the cleverer, prettier, more outgoing one. How she persuaded our cousins to go running off with her, leaving me out of their games.

These are petty things and any decision I might make is not about childhood resentment; this is not about retribution versus forgiveness. Just that my sister and I have never particularly got along. Nonetheless...What sort of person will it make me if I say no?

I focus on my breathing. Elaine counts me through the samples she is taking. "Two left," she says, her voice artificially patient, as if coaxing an unreasonable child.

With her brisk efficiency, she is not someone I can imagine liking in other circumstances. Just as my sister and I would never have become friends. Love is different to friendship, and the former does not necessarily require the latter, yet I have no idea what definition of love would encompass my feelings towards my sister. It isn't that I'm indifferent to her ill health and shortened life expectancy, just as I am not indifferent to the many flavours of suffering in the world. Neither am I responsible for putting things right.

"All done," Elaine says, her voice nursery-teacher bright. She removes the needle and deftly places a cotton wool ball in its place, applying pressure over the puncture site. I think of the pressure of expectation, building like a deep-sea dive, the assumption by my sister and mother, and quite likely wider opinion too: how could someone not do this for her sister if she has the chance?

Elaine asks me to take over pressing the cotton wool down, and she stretches clear tape firmly across it.

"Well done," she says as if my endurance is a cause for congratulations. No doubt she will be glad to be shot of me. She turns to fuss with paperwork and samples, leaving me free to depart. I stand, start to walk away, and think about how today is the very simplest of the steps; it can only get worse. All at once, a bolt of dizziness strikes, hard and fast, the world blurring. Darting thoughts tell me I won't make the waiting room, can't even retreat back to the glowing green chair, so I do what I've learned to do, and I plonk myself down on the floor, my knees up and wide, head lowered between them.

"Are you alright?" the Elaine woman says. A stupid question; I am not particularly partial to sitting on hard, dusty lino. "Would you like some water?" A plastic cup is pressed into my hand. I raise my head enough to sip, and the dizziness worsens. I bend forward as far as I can get.

"Just sit quietly for a while," Elaine says. I have no choice but to obey. I remain here, sweating and shivering, nausea pressing. I gaze at the patterned flooring, whose geometric lines keep undulating. Elaine will be getting impatient. The queue in the waiting room will be lengthening. The more I worry about a quick recovery, the longer it will take. I lift my head and sip the water again, trying to quell the queasiness.

I remember...

How I hated rice pudding at school. How the teachers insisted on clear plates, and my throat constricted, and my eyes filled with tears, knowing I couldn't bear to eat this disgusting slop, but I couldn't bear to be told off either. And sometimes Elaine would surreptitiously swap her empty bowl for my full one, eating it for me, the single act of kindness which stands out amongst the many examples of her being mean. Of course, she was always hungry and actually liked the milky puddings I couldn't stand. But still.

"Any better?" Elaine asks.

"A bit." I only have to walk a few steps to get out of here. "I should be OK," I say, and I stand slowly, and Elaine takes my arm and accompanies me the first few yards. I make it to a chair by the window, where I sit and allow everything to settle. I think through what has just happened. If the simple fact of giving blood can fill me with dizzy panic, how much worse will the subsequent tests and procedures be? Never mind the endgame.

The primal core of my being cries out that I wish for my body to remain intact. I could overcome my terror, presumably, if it was my own health at risk. But it isn't. It is only my sister, the sister against whom I argued and competed my way through childhood, both of us feeling nothing but relief when we went our separate ways. We abide by the conventions of card sending and occasional phone calls and meeting up at Mum's for Christmas, but neither of us would miss the other if she weren't there, not really.

Survival instincts are dead set against this act of self-harm, and I doubt she'd do this for me the other way.

I am pushed up against the limits of sibling love, all of the arguments pointing in one direction, and yet... She's my sister. She shares my DNA and history; she has helped shape who I have become.

I sit quietly, sipping chlorine-flavoured water and inhaling the sharp, dank smell of hospital waiting rooms, and I think how massively convenient it will be if the match fails.

7. Angel Eyes

Jenifer Moore

She wasn't there when he fell. She'd lost sight of him briefly, turning her attention to the baby as she must have done umpteen times that day. Grady was teething – a dribbling, fretful ball of red-gummed pain, wriggling on the bed of towels beside her. She'd lain him down just minutes before, full of milk and sleep, but already he was awake again, preparing to bawl.

Eva looked down the beach to where Patrick stood, bucket in one hand and that ridiculous Union Jack flag in the other. He was staring intently into a pool of water, searching for crabs, most likely. Perhaps later, when her husband arrived to take the baby off her hands, she'd take him down to the proper rock pools. They could look for prawns and anemones and those tiny starfish that loitered in the shallows.

Eva nestled the baby into her shoulder and hurried back up the sand to the abandoned pushchair – to the remains of their picnic lunch, lying limp and sandy in the too-warm Tupperware box. A lone carrot stick still clung defiantly to the lid. Maybe that would keep him quiet for a bit.

"Has Grady got the grumps? Mummy give you some carrot to chew on?"

The baby paused for a moment, weighing up his response before letting rip with a fresh wave of misery. Back down the beach they went, back to the little blue sun shelter that was their prison for the afternoon. She propped him up against the spare pillow she'd brought from home, wedged in tight between her leg and the sloping back of the tent, and presented him with the promised carrot stick. He grabbed at it with his fat pink fist, lifting it up to the red wailing 'O' of his mouth. The effect was instantaneous. The sounds of sea and shouting children drifted back into being as he sucked and slobbered in silence. His new-found contentment lasted all of eight seconds, which was exactly how long it took her to scan the length and breadth of the beach, a tight ball of panic rising in her throat.

"Patrick? Patrick? Patrick!"

Already, she was up and running, the baby bouncing against her chest, screaming for his lost carrot, which had slipped from his mouth and lay somewhere on the sand behind them. She was still looking as she ran, still searching desperately for a sign of bright green swimming trunks, for a glimpse of the orange bucket or plastic Union Jack. Small clusters of children swam in and out of focus: a little girl with blonde ringlets patted at her sandcastle; a sunburnt boy hurled a ball towards his father's cricket bat; two teenagers dragged a black and white dinghy down towards the water's edge.

"Patrick!"

There was the pool. Another child's spade floated forgotten on the surface of the water.

"Patrick!"

"Are you looking for your little boy?" asked a paunchy man in blue speedos. She spun around, the words tumbling out of her in a jumbled rush.

"You've found him it's Patrick, I just turned my back for a where is he?"

"Last time I saw him, he was heading off towards the rock pools with his bucket. Come on, I'll help you look. Don't worry, love, I'm sure he's fine. You know what boys are like."

"But he's not allowed on the rocks. Not on his own. He knows he's not allowed…" She was weeping now, great panicky sobs choking in her chest. She hugged the baby tight.

"Patrick!" The man was calling his name, too, as they ran.

A sliver of red, white and blue winked at them from the dark granite rocks.

"That's his flag." It lay deserted on a sharp ridge about three metres from the edge of the sand.

"You stay there, love," said the man. "Look after the baby."

He set off, clambering across the rocks in his bare feet. Twice, he caught his ankle on a jagged edge and cursed. From where Eva stood on the sand, she could make out a thin trickle of blood dribbling down the white flesh of his foot. He paused for a moment when he reached the flag, staring out towards the incoming sea, before dropping down out of sight.

"Have you found him?" she called. "Patrick? Is he there? What's happening?"

The world stood still. A lone surfer lingered indefinitely on the crest of a wave. Even the baby had fallen quiet. But then the man reappeared on top of the rocks. Alone. In his hand, he carried a bright orange bucket. A howling cry came tearing out of her, vibrating through her whole body as people came running. She felt someone lifting the baby from her arms. And then the man was beside her again, a shy hand on her elbow and soft words buzzing round under the wings of her cry. There were kind voices, hurried phone calls and more running footsteps. Somewhere overhead, a helicopter whirled and fretted through the cloudless sky as a towel-wrapped woman pressed a cup of hot sugary tea into her hand. And then her husband was there – more questions, a fresh round of blame.

Five whole hours they searched, as the heat dripped slowly out of the sun. Curious holidaymakers drifted through the scene; a sweaty uniformed policeman whispering crackled nothing into his radio. Eva sat with the empty orange bucket, staring hollow-eyed at the faded price label on the handle, her mind a dull orange nothing.

When the first shout came, she was too deep inside her own grief and guilt to notice. It was the second one that caught her, rippling up the beach on a wave of smiles and back-slapping.

"They've found him," came the cry. "He's OK. They've found him."

Still, she clutched the bucket.

"The little boy," they shouted. "He's safe."

And now she was running. Running towards the sweaty policeman with the blanketed figure bundled up in his arms.

"Patrick!" Her feet pounded the wet sand. "Oh, Patrick."

Somewhere behind her, the baby began to wail.

No one had been able to tell them anything.

"It was an angel," Patrick said, smiling. "My angel."

The policeman shrugged his shoulders. "Like I said, there he was on the rock, safe and sound. We scoured every inch of that stretch of coastline. Beats me. Still, he's a plucky little soul."

"An angel," Patrick insisted.

He clung stubbornly to his story all the way back from the hospital, long after they'd stopped asking him.

"He had white eyes, and his hair was like fire. It wasn't hot, though. He let me touch it."

"You know you mustn't wander off on your own," she told him. "We were so worried. I thought..." But she couldn't tell him what she'd thought. She only knew she never wanted to think it again.

"And his hands were like ice. Sort of see-through and shiny."

"Patrick."

"And his wings were... actually, I don't think he had any."

"I don't know what I'd have done..."

"I wonder how he flies without any wings? We were right up high in the sky."

"My precious boy…"

"And you were all there on the beach. You were holding my bucket, and Grady was doing 'peepo' with a big fat lady. I couldn't see Daddy. But I saw the policeman. He carried me up the beach after the angel brought me back."

"I should never have left you on your own."

"But he couldn't see the angel. Only I could."

"I'd never have forgiven myself."

Patrick smiled at the memory, tracing a dripping face on the steamed-up window with his finger. Eva watched him in the mirror, watched the figure emerging through the white, with its wild flaming hair and strange blank eyes fixed on her son. A shiver of ice rippled down the back of her sundress, and she twisted round in her seat to wipe the glass clean.

He was sleeping soundly when she came upstairs to bed that night. Expert after expert had assured her, he was fine. There'd been tests and scans, and there were no complications. And yet… She opened the window – just a crack to keep him from overheating – and stood there, watching his eyes flicker beneath their pale lids, studying the rise and fall of his chest through the thin summer sheet. She could have stayed there forever. But then, from next door came the shrill scream of the baby as he woke to find himself alone in the darkened bedroom. She sighed.

"Night night, Patrick," she whispered, closing the door carefully behind her.

"Night night, my angel."

She dreamed he was flying, the sea a blue-green flag beneath his outstretched arms, rippling in the breeze. She dreamed of helicopters buzzing insect-like across the sky, circling, searching. White, white eyes.

Where had they come from? A blur of flame. And then he was falling. An orange bucket. A black and white dinghy bobbing on a wave. Falling. Falling.

And just like that, she dreamed him back into his own room. He was standing on the bed, watching the white angel eyes of a taxi through a gap in the curtains. The eyes blinked, and he tugged the curtains aside to reveal a dripping face waiting in the misted glass.

"No," Eva moaned in her sleep, willing him away from the window. But even as she flung an arm against her husband's sleeping spine, she knew it was only a dream. It had to be. Even when she heard the soft creak of her son's bedroom window stretching wide, she knew it couldn't be real. And the subtle change in his breathing as he hauled himself up onto the sill – that was all in her sleeping head.

Please, please let it be a dream.

"Patrick!" Eva screamed as he leaned out into the night, searching for his angel. "Patrick!"

She wasn't there when he fell.

8. The King's Shilling

Hamish MacNeil

The two boys lay in the dim, grey room, listening to the clamour and commotion without. Beyond the thin curtains, a constant migration of men and munitions tramped up gangplanks onto waiting vessels, while inside the boarding house, a similar procession of soldiers and sailors with kit bags and rifles could be heard on every stair and landing. Soon, it would be their turn to embark on the war in France to do their duty for king and country.

"I wish–" said William.

"Don't," interrupted Henry, pulling the counterpane up to his neck and turning away.

"I just wish," repeated William, laying a hand on Henry's shoulder and gently turning him back, "I wish we could exchange rings; bear some token of each other; a reminder of our love. How many lads out there are leaving wives behind or are at least promised officially with the gift of a ring? They will all have photographs in their pockets of a sweetheart, too; that's tangible, at least. But what can we have of each other in the months to come?"

"I said don't. What's the use of wishing? I wish this bloody war had never started, I–" Henry sighed in anguish and flung back the counterpane, sitting up and swinging his legs off the narrow bed. The action caused his shiny dog tags to jingle against his chest. He turned to look at William, holding a tag between thumb and forefinger.

"We could swap these," he said excitedly. "Then we could belong to each other, wear a constant reminder."

"And literally take each other's names!" said William, taking his own tags from around his neck.

The two boys held out their dog tags to one another, solemn and silent amidst the hubbub of the harbour.

"Should there be some kind of ceremony?" asked William. "Should we say something?"

Henry took William's left hand in his and turned the palm up like an oyster shell.

"I give you these tags as a token of me; keep them against your heart until we can meet again, for I am yours, and you are mine, from this day until our last days." He placed the silver discs that bore his name, number, rank, religion and blood type into the open hand and closed William's fingers around them. He looked into the other boy's face and held out his own left hand.

"Now," he said, a bright smile on his face, "I am Miller, William, Private, Somerset Light Infantry," and he pulled the chain over his head, pressing the tags to his breastbone.

"And I am proud to be Ousby, Henry, Private, Devonshire regiment." He held Henry's gaze for half a minute, not sure how long it would be until he could do so again, then he forced himself up off the bed. "Right, Bill, we'd best get ourselves dressed. The Hun awaits!"

"Here, we'd better swap jackets and hats, too – the insignia," said the new William Miller, "it's a good job we're the same size, eh?"

"Bloody thing doesn't fit me properly anyway," said the new Private Ousby, "I'll probably look much better in your gear."

"Look better for who?" Henry gave him an indignant punch on the arm. "You'd better be faithful over there," he admonished, "and mind you don't get any bullet holes in it, neither."

Henry sank down onto the muddy board and set his mess tin next to him, the ration of bully beef and some indeterminate, rancid vegetable forgotten for the moment. He wiped his cold, filthy fingers on the underside of his lapel and carefully opened the letter.

"Letter from your sweetheart?" said a voice from a corner of the dugout. Henry was too cold and tired to acknowledge it. "What's 'er name, Miller? You got a photograph?"

Henry focused on the pattern of neat letters, words written at a desk in a quiet house in England, writing like his used to be; words that spoke of farming and village life, where the sun wasn't obscured by mud and death and clouds of gas, where cattle lowed in the evenings, and grown men didn't moan and cry out all night only to fall ever silent by morning; where the tap-tap-tap of woodpeckers didn't set one's teeth on edge like the rat-tat-tat of the machine guns that cut through trees and steel and bone better than any beak.

"I'm just curious, see, Miller, cos when I first met you, I thought you was a queer."

"Leave it out, Carter," said another weary voice.

Henry looked up. He fumbled the letter back into its envelope and slowly unbuttoned his top pocket. Bill had kept a picture of his sister in his tunic; she shared his fine features. He held it out to Carter, now, without a word.

"Very nice, Miller, I'm impressed. Must have been a small village you came from, eh?" drawled Carter.

"Leave him be, Carter. I want to get some rest."

"I'm only teasing the lad, Jenkins. You lie there, and I'll nip over to the Boche and ask them to cease hostilities for a few hours so you can get your beauty sleep." He gave the photograph back, and Henry returned it to his pocket, along with the letter from William's mother. He picked up his mess tin and set about eating the cold tinned beef; there was no pleasure to be derived from the meal, just the feeling of a less empty belly. As his right arm and jaw mechanically dealt with the food, his thoughts turned to William and the letters he must be receiving. What were his family doing? How were they coping without him? And William, was he in some cold, wet hole this very minute, trying to digest his rations? Had he even received any in the last few days? Was he under fire? Was he…

Henry balanced the mess tin on his knees and rubbed his chest as if he had heartburn, feeling the comforting edges of Williams's dog tags against his skin.

Another soldier came down the log steps with a rifle and mess tin and news: "We're leaving at dawn," he said, "going to relieve the Devonshires'."

A grotesque dawn chorus from the big guns behind covered the movement of the troops the next morning. The Somerset Light Infantry squirmed along miles of narrow trench, slipping on wooden walkways or knee-deep in ooze, never sure what they were treading underfoot, drowned rats or the limbs of dismembered countrymen. Henry had once been knocked down by a shell exploding fifty yards away, shrapnel pelting his Brodie helmet and covering his prone body. When he had come to, he clawed his fingers across his face to remove the dirt and debris and found himself staring at an eyeball he had assumed was his own.

As they neared their destination, a position on a narrow stretch of no man's land, machine gun fire from the Germans frequently animated the bags at the top of the trench. Henry's company crouched lower as they scurried along past the bodies of Devonshire soldiers lying and sitting dead or asleep along the sides of the trench. Henry searched each haggard face for the cheeks, nose and mouth he knew so well. Finally, they came to a halt, and the sergeant gave out the orders. Henry was told to find a dugout and get some rest before the night watch, so he turned quickly and hurried to make enquiries.

"Ousby? Try over there."

"Sergeant? Private William Miller, sir. I'm looking for private Ousby." Henry snapped a smart salute in spite of his fatigue.

"That lad will be getting a medal, I shouldn't wonder. He was part of a sortie last night. Made it back but shot up something terrible. He's in the hospital tent awaiting transportation."

Sick to his stomach, hoping it didn't show, a mask of mud and hardship hiding his pallor, Henry stumbled in a daze to the busy hospital tent. A nurse stood by the side of the door, her white apron more like a cardinal's red gown, as she wiped her forehead with the back of a red-black hand.

"Excuse me? Do you have news of Henry Ousby?" he managed, his throat dry and his deafening heartbeat the only sound he could hear.

The nurse straightened and said she would fetch the doctor, then slipped through the door of the tent. After an agonising wait, the tent flap lifted again, and a doctor emerged. Henry stood to attention automatically, and the doctor looked kindly at him for a moment, then reached out a hand and gripped Henry's shoulder.

"I'm sorry," he said. "We patched him up, and he should have pulled through; he had lost a lot of blood, but he was still strong." The doctor looked down for a moment and took a deep breath. "He reacted to the transfusion we gave him; blood must have been the wrong type. Maybe the supplies were mislabelled, or perhaps his tags were printed incorrectly. These things happen, I'm afraid. I'm sorry. He was a brave lad."

The doctor gave Henry's shoulder another squeeze, then returned to his duties. Henry's legs buckled beneath him, and he staggered blindly through the mud, clutching his chest.

9. The Lavender Witches

Willow Hewett

I took a deep breath as I stood at the gate, staring up at the small, crumbling cottage in front of me. Green foliage had taken over most of the front garden, entwining and weaving with one another, covering every possible part of the earth and making the garden appear unkempt. Parts of the cottage walls had begun to crumble due to age and the lack of anyone available to repair them, but I didn't mind. A smile spread across my lips as I pushed back the rotten wooden gate, colliding with a large brick that had come loose from the wall beside me. My shoes crunched beneath my feet as I fumbled for my new key, overjoyed at the prospect of finally owning my own home, which I had been saving for since I was in my early twenties.

Wildflowers had sprouted among the overgrown poison ivy, leaving only the dusty path unspoiled by Mother Nature. The sun glinted off the cloudy-looking windows, which appeared to have been cleaned recently. I didn't mind the state of the place. It was mine.

My hands shook with excitement as my thumb rubbed the smooth metal of the key. I stood in front of the blue-painted door, which had age-related chipping on the sides and stroked the wood with my fingertips. It was accompanied by an old iron lion's head knocker that hung to the left from a broken screw that had come loose from the rotting door.

I looked down and saw that my luggage had arrived ahead of me at the request of the town council, who had asked me to buy the property, claiming that I would be the ideal candidate to join the town of

Axbridge, and I eagerly accepted the offer, hoping that I had made the right decision and that I would meet some new friends.

The town council was run by the husbands' wives of the quiet little town, who hoped to attract more like-minded women to help bring the area to life and win the title of the prettiest town of the year.

The town was hidden in the countryside, surrounded by fields and nature. It was just what I needed to get over my past. I needed peace and quiet, and this was the perfect place to find it. The cottages all appeared to be the same, crammed together side by side, with only small gaps for lanes large enough to pass a small car through. There was an organic produce shop in the town, and next to it was a post office full of knickknacks and drab, dusty ornaments that had most likely been there since it first opened. Only the regulars knew about the town's one pub for socialising, which was hidden up a lane behind the post office. The pub was stuffy and old, crammed with antique farming equipment hung on the walls as decoration, demonstrating how old the town was.

When I heard a noise coming from the bushes, I was startled. As I moved my gaze through the shrubbery, I noticed a woman's face emerge, grinning from ear to ear.

"At long last, I have a neighbour." She exclaimed as she pushed her way through the space between the cottage and the bush. "I'm Daisy. I moved here six months ago. You'll enjoy it here. It's peaceful and serene, and I adore it!"

She appeared to be my age and had long blonde hair that fell past her hips. She looked as if she'd just gotten out of bed as she slurped her morning brew, her gaze fixed on me over her mug. She was still in her nightgown and hadn't bothered to put on shoes, so her feet were bare and caked in mud from her garden.

I smiled back and nodded. "Yes, I've only recently received the keys. My name is Fiona."

When I told her why I moved to Axbridge, she laughed and said it was the same reason she moved. The town council had also asked her to move here, which irritated me because I wasn't the only one they wanted.

After a week, I was thankful for Daisy's company. She checked in on me every day to make sure I was okay. The town council had also paid me a visit and brought me home-warming gifts that included a small handmade doll made of straw from a nearby farm, a metal mug made by the town blacksmith, and a pot of herbs grown in each of their gardens. The gifts were unusual to me, but they were appreciated, nonetheless. I spent days cleaning and organising the cottage so that I could live comfortably. Daisy decided to come over and help on the fourth day. We talked and laughed, and I could tell we were becoming friends. She stayed for dinner and then helped me clean up.

"What are your thoughts on the town council?" Daisy asked.

I didn't know what to say and didn't want to offend her in case she knew any of them, but the gifts they'd given me weighed heavily on my mind. They were too strange to be normal, so I hid them beneath my bed to keep visitors from asking questions about them.

She noticed my hesitation. "Go on, you can say it. I find them rather strange, too."

I breathed a sigh of relief. "There's just something off about them. I don't want to be rude, as it was very kind of them to help me with this place, but I'm so glad that you're here to keep me company."

Daisy giggled as she dipped her hands into the soapy water to wash up. "I know what you mean. Before you moved here, I was starting to pack up as I was just so bored. Don't get me wrong, this place is beautiful, and there's so much to see, but it's missing a friend. Someone I could connect with and talk to about silly things that aren't to do with homemade bread or the newest ale they have in the pub."

I grabbed a dishcloth and began drying the plates, lost in my own thoughts, trying to figure out how I felt about them. "They gave me some presents, but they aren't ordinary presents. It's odd things like an herb pot and a handmade doll."

Daisy nodded in agreement. "I had the same gifts, but the doll was custom-made to look like me. I didn't want to offend anyone, so I accepted them and hid them in the fireplace."

"Odd behaviour, isn't it? Or is it just us because we're city girls, and this is the norm around here?" I asked, more to myself than to Daisy, as I tried to make sense of the situation.

She chuckled and yanked at my arm with her soapy, wet hand. "Let's go sit outside for a while. Get some sun before it gets dark."

I let her drag me outside and usher me to a scruffy-looking bench left behind by the previous owners. She sat down beside me, looking across the road at the next cottage. An elderly woman stood outside her window, glaring down at us as if we were trespassing on her property. She vanished from view a few seconds later, leaving both of us staring at each other and laughing.

"What was that all about?" I asked.

Daisy shrugged, clearly uneasy about the situation. "I'm not sure. I've never met her, but I've seen her squall around, peering into other people's gardens and cursing them loudly, especially those with lavender growing in them." She looked up, and her eyes widened in surprise.

"Oh, no, she's heading this way."

When I looked up, I saw the old lady hunched over and scraping her walking stick across the path to get to us. Her skin was as wrinkly as old tree bark, and her bony knuckles poked through her paper-thin skin as she clutched her stick. She bashed my gate open with force, and we stood there, mouths agape, staring at her as she slithered towards us like a snake eyeing its prey. Her raggedy old clothes dangled from her skeletal frame. Her stockings appeared to be too big for her leg, wrinkling up at the knee.

She stopped just in front of us and spoke in a raspy tone. "You're both new here, aren't you?"

I raised my eyebrows at her, unsure what she wanted. "You could say that, yes."

The woman's face became solemn, and she leaned in. "Beware the houses dripping in purple."

I drew back, smelling the whiskey on her breath. "What exactly do you mean?"

She began to backtrack slowly, back onto the path, her dark brown, menacing eyes fixed on us. "You'll find out soon enough when the full moon bathes the town in silver light. Don't say I didn't warn you, missies."

The woman hobbled up the path, her stick clanging against the gate as she threw it open again, causing the wall to tremble violently. We sat in silence, taking in what the elderly lady had just said, unsure of what she was trying to tell us. The elderly lady then stopped in the middle of the road, staring to the left at something out of sight. We kept watching as a woman from the town council emerged from behind the bush, cruelly smiling and stopping inches from the old woman's face. We couldn't understand what they were saying, but they appeared to be arguing about something. She stopped when she noticed us staring and walked towards us, leaving the old woman, who was shaking with fear, behind. She looked like she was from the 1970s, with her long, beaded hair and flowery, flowing dress that reached her ankles. She wore a lot of bangles on each wrist, and her fingers were covered in strange, symbolic tattoos that had no meaning. Her face was long and oval, with bright red lipstick on her small, pouty lips that protruded more than her button nose.

"Hello!" She called out as she bounced up the path. "Lovely day, isn't it?" She didn't bother waiting for us to respond. Instead, she continued to speak quickly. "I'm Andrea, and I'm the chairman of the town committee. I'd like to formally introduce myself to our newest neighbour." She reached out and grabbed my hand, shaking it vigorously. "Welcome, Fiona. I hope you've settled in nicely."

I nodded slowly, removing my hand from her clammy fingers. "I have, indeed. Thank you very much."

She moved her hands to her hips and brushed her long hair away from her face. "Excellent, excellent. That's exactly what I wanted to hear. Daisy, I'm glad you're here as well because I wanted to invite you to our next committee meeting tomorrow evening at the town hall. There will be homemade cakes and hot beverages for you to enjoy while we discuss our next summer fair plans."

Daisy was taken aback and turned away from Andrea, trying to hide her disgusted expression. "I appreciate the invitation, but it's not really my style."

Andrea, enraged, shook her head. "That's nonsense, my dear. It's your thing; you just don't realise it. I'll see you at 6 pm sharp. Please don't keep me waiting."

She dashed back down the path before Daisy could say anything, her flowery dress flapping in the breeze, revealing another tattoo in the shape of a crow on her ankle.

"Wow, wasn't she a force to be reckoned with?" I asked, breaking our stunned silence. "I'm curious as to why she didn't invite me as well."

Daisy looked at me, her eyes wide with terror. "I won't be able to attend something like that. It's just not my style, and before you know it, I'm making homemade herb bread like them."

I stifled a laugh and clutched her hand tightly. "I'll accompany you so you're not alone."

"That would be fantastic, thank you." She muttered quietly as she looked off into the sunset.

The next day flew by, and it was time to go to the town hall, where the entire town committee would be droning on about boring fairs and the next best bread recipe. I walked up the hall steps with Daisy, nervous about what was behind those doors. Daisy was clutching my arm, so I knew she felt the same way. When the doors opened, a beaming Andrea greeted us.

Her smile dropped when she saw me approaching with Daisy. "No, no, no. Daisy, you were meant to come alone." She seethed, her eyes wild with rage. "Fiona, I'm sorry, but it's not your turn yet. It's Daisy's turn. Your time will come soon."

Before I could respond, she yanked Daisy's arm away from mine and dragged her up the last few steps to the hall. She gave me one last look, shaking her head in disappointment, and dragged a terrified Daisy into the hall, slamming the door violently behind her. I stood there stunned, going over what had just happened in my head. It didn't make any sense. As I walked home alone, rage welled up inside of me. I looked across at the old lady's cottage and noticed her curtain twitching. I brushed it aside and dashed up the garden path, slamming the front door shut behind me.

For days, I waited for Daisy to come round, but she never turned up. I decided to pluck up the courage to go to hers instead, hoping she'd be there and gossip with me about what it was like on the committee. I walked slowly up her garden path, noticing that her little cottage was beginning to grow lavender around the walls and front door, bringing colour to her home. I rapped on her door and waited for her to answer. There was no one in.

For weeks after that, I waited and waited for her to appear, and after a while, I stopped watching from my window and got busy fixing up the cottage. Daisy didn't show up again until the lavender that had engulfed her cottage and taken over her garden had bloomed. I was putting up a curtain rod when I noticed Daisy, Andrea, and a few other women walking up the road, laughing and chatting as they went. I jumped off the stool and dashed outside to greet her, but I ground to a standstill when I noticed how much Daisy had changed. Like an old oak tree, her skin was gnarled and gaunt. Her once-shiny blonde hair had become scruffy, and beads had been inserted, just like Andrea's. Her clothes were starting to look less like hers and more like Andrea's. She, like the others, wore the handmade doll she was given attached to her belt.

When she noticed me, she smiled. Her smile ended at her lips and never reached her eyes. "Good morning, Fiona. We were on our way to your house to invite you to the upcoming committee meeting."

The terror that I felt coursed through my veins as I stared into Daisy's cold, foreboding eyes. I shook my head and stepped back from them.

Andrea stepped towards me. "Don't be shy, Fiona. You'll be fine. We shall come and collect you tomorrow at six. Make sure you're ready."

"No!" I yelled and dashed away from them. I slammed my door shut and peered out the window, knowing they'd be discussing my sudden outburst. In my head, I knew it was irrational to believe that something had happened to Daisy at the town hall, but in my gut, I knew there was something seriously wrong with this place. I watched as they walked away, giggling at each other and peering over at my cottage. The old lady's curtain twitched again, and I remembered what she'd said.

'Beware the houses dripping with purple.'
Was she talking about lavender?

After dark, I decided to go to each of the committee members' houses and see if they had lavender growing on them. They had all swathed their homes in lavender. I finally understood what the old lady had meant. I got home and didn't sleep at all that night, knowing that the committee meeting was the next day. I paced up and down my living room until sunrise. A small knock on the door interrupted my thoughts. I slowly opened the door to find a doll that was an exact replica of me on the floor, next to a lit candle on top of a strange-looking symbol that had been drawn on the floor in chalk.

Then I noticed lavender sprouting up around my front door and garden, just like it had at Daisy's. The hairs on the back of my neck stood on end as I stepped into my garden and looked at the purple buds growing from the walls. I noticed a shadow in Daisy's window and looked up to see Daisy smiling down at me while holding a bouquet of lavender flowers. I knew right away that this wasn't the Daisy I knew, and I knew my time would come to an end when the lavender bloomed fully, and the full moon rose at the witching hour. I checked the calendar on the wall and noticed that there was a full moon tonight. My stomach began to churn, warning me that they would be coming for me after dark.

10. Juggler

Fenja Hill

Kelly sat at the back of the room, tilting her chair and leaning back against the wall. She chewed her gum loudly enough to ensure that the girls sitting near her could hear and know that she was a rebel, but not loudly enough for Mr Collins to hear her and throw her out again. If she was thrown out of another class, her father would take the belt to her again, and the last set of bruises had only just faded. It wasn't easy keeping the balance between trying to make friends by being rebellious and entertaining at school and not getting a belting. Last night, she watched an old episode of the Catherine Tate show again and wished she had the courage to be as smart and funny as Lauren, the brilliant schoolgirl character. But no one in real life could get away with that sort of behaviour.

Kelly was an extra.

In every film about high school, there were two or three that you recognised, that were at the centre of the plot, wore the best clothes, had cool boyfriends, and survived the serial killer while the extras dropped by the wayside; always interchangeable extras. So, the three key characters would be in a classroom or a gym or at a dance or a party, and there would be twenty others occupying all the other seats or dancing or whatever–the extras. If one of them disappeared, no one would notice or care. Like Kelly. It wasn't that Kelly was bullied or picked on; she just didn't matter. She didn't have a best friend. She hung out with some of the other girls, went to the same parties and events simply because everyone knew they were happening, and nobody needed an invitation. She talked to them and tried to say things they would remember, often by making them laugh. She'd had a sort of weird success a couple of times when she'd heard Annabelle or Melissa repeating something funny that she'd said to them, but they didn't give her credit and probably didn't even remember where they'd heard it.

She knew Ryan had walked into the classroom because all the girls stopped talking, and there were one or two giggles, but she didn't turn her head to look. Mr Collins said something sarcastic about Ryan being kind enough to join them and then told them all to leave the drama room and go down to the main hall. Today's lesson was to be something different from the usual stuff.

Trailing along the corridor, almost at the back of the group, Kelly swung round and slapped away a hand that had reached out and grabbed her left buttock. Her response was automatic, she hardly noticed herself doing it anymore and didn't even look to see who it was, although it still really pissed her off. And she still didn't properly understand it. Kelly was an extra, pretty much invisible; she wasn't pretty like Annabelle and Melissa or clever like Jasmine, and yet there was something about her that pulled the boys in. Something they wanted to touch, to feel. Hardly a day went by when one or other of the boys in her class didn't 'accidentally' brush against her getting on or off the bus, reaching up to their locker, or walking past her desk in a classroom. She had tried wearing different clothes, doing up more buttons on her blouse, never making eye contact with any of the boys, but nothing stopped them. It wasn't that they fancied her, liked her in a real way. She couldn't remember the last time one of them had actually spoken to her. If one of the boys genuinely liked her, they would have been falling over themselves to ask her out, but that never happened. Almost every boy in the class had asked Annabelle and Melissa out, and both had refused them all. Everyone knew what they were waiting for; Ryan. Every girl in the class wanted him, but it was understood that when he finally did decide, it would be either Annabelle or Melissa, he asked out. Kelly wondered briefly what they would think if they knew about what had happened yesterday.

Yesterday, Kelly had been the first person into the form room in the morning for registration. She had been standing at the window, gazing across to the sports field and wondering whether she could find a way to avoid double games, when a hand had reached around from behind and cupped her left breast. She jumped a mile and was starting to swing round, hand raised to slap as hard as she could when she caught a glimpse of her reflection and that of the perpetrator in the window. And saw who it was. Of course, he'd done this sort of thing a few times before, but never when they were completely alone. He was one of the ones who liked to brush past her getting onto the bus or drop a book close to her and touch her leg on the way down to pick it up. Mind racing, she continued the turn but stepped forward so that she was nose to nose with Ryan, staring into his eyes, and, instead of the stinging slap she had first intended, her hand met his cheek softly and stayed there for a moment. Kelly had never done any of this stuff before, but she had seen enough films and read enough books to know exactly how it should go. She could become a real person, no longer an extra. Whoever had Ryan would not be invisible.

Kelly took both of Ryan's hands, now hanging limply at his sides and placed one on each of her breasts. She didn't take her eyes from Ryan's. He was grinning now as though he couldn't believe his luck. He was also starting to move his hands, exploring her body.

She waited a few seconds and then stepped back, out of reach.

"That's it. Enough. If you want more, you can have it if you ask me out on a real date, like a proper girlfriend. You can have whatever you want." She wasn't entirely sure about that, but she was willing to do quite a lot to become less of a shadow, and she thought she could even tolerate sex if he insisted. She knew he didn't like her, wasn't attracted to her. It was the same for him as for the other boys, something she couldn't place didn't understand but now realised that she could use. She had something he wanted, and he could help her find something she craved.

"Think about it." She turned away and walked over to her desk as the rest of the class started to drift in.

What would the other girls think if they knew? They'd call her a tart and worse. But they'd be jealous, too. Ryan didn't want them, and he did want Kelly, even if it wasn't in the way she would have liked.

They reached the hall and sat around the wall on benches. In various places around the huge room, bits of equipment had been set up, and there were five strangers hanging around in a group. They were wearing multi-coloured sparkly leggings and black t-shirts with their names on them.

Mr Collins called them all together and explained that today, they were being given an opportunity to learn some circus skills. For the next ten minutes, the guests would demonstrate different skills, and then they could all have a go themselves. There would be nothing dangerous, no high-wire walking, but it should be interesting and fun and might broaden their horizons, and their perception of what drama was all about.

The demonstration started. There was a man walking on stilts; he made it look really easy, but Kelly suspected that was not the case. There was a young woman riding a unicycle and occasionally juggling oranges at the same time. Now and then, she would throw one up to the man on the stilts, and he would catch it and flick it back to her, but she never lost her balance or the rhythm of the juggling. There was another man spinning plates on poles and someone else doing all sorts of clever stuff with hula hoops. One other man was juggling very slowly with things that looked like giant versions of the pins you knock down at ten-pin bowling. Kelly heard someone say they were called clubs.

They all wandered round the hall, watching. Before the ten minutes were up, Kelly could see that a few of the girls were already trying to hula, with varying degrees of success. Shelley was managing to keep two hoops going at the same time while Annabelle was giggling too much to even keep one up. Because Annabelle was there, some of the boys joined that group. Other boys were asking to have a go at the stilt-walking, and a few more pairs of stilts had been brought out. The boys were having even less success with this than Anabelle with the hula hoops.

Kelly couldn't see anything that appealed. She spotted Ryan trying to ride the unicycle and moved away. If anything was going to happen, he needed to come to her; she didn't want him to think she was desperate.

Kelly wandered over to the man juggling with the clubs. He nodded to her as she joined the small group watching him. As he juggled, he was talking, explaining. There were spare clubs on the floor and a couple of the boys had picked some up and were trying to follow the instructions. And failing. Kelly joined the laughter of the others who were watching. The man – his t-shirt said his name was Tom – was explaining about catch and release and the rhythm.

The clubs were sparkling, multi-coloured, glittering under the fluorescent lights of the hall. Everyone was watching them and listening to Tom's words. Kelly tried to count the clubs, but the speed and the sparkles made them all blur into one beautiful rainbow. If she couldn't even work out how many there were, how could she learn to do it? She thought for a while. The clubs were beautiful, but they were just the tools. Surely what mattered was the hands, getting the movements right? She listened again to what Tom was saying about catch and release, but it seemed too complicated.

Kelly tore her eyes from the sparkling magic and focused. She watched Tom's hands. At first, she was only watching one, but then she moved slowly round until she was standing directly in front of him and worked hard to bring both hands into her line of sight. She listened to Tom's words, and she watched. The first thing she realised was that there was actually very little movement. It was all in small twists and turns and flicks of the wrists and the swift opening and closing of fingers around the clubs.

She watched.

Around her, there was laughter and an occasional cheer as others attempted the various skills, but her eyes stayed on Tom's hands. She could see the rhythm. Her own hands, although empty, were involuntarily beginning to mirror his and she could feel the smooth flow of the actions. It wasn't difficult. It was like reading. At first, you struggle to spell out the words, one letter at a time, and then suddenly, it all comes together, and you're reading a book.

She watched.

Tom increased the speed of his juggling, and Kelly went with him without even thinking about it. Her peripheral vision told her that the clubs were a rainbow blur. Tom had also introduced an adjustment into the pattern so that every fourth club was thrown slightly higher than the others, and Kelly knew that she was throwing her invisible clubs in exactly the same way. She heard a snigger next to her and realised that one of the boys was mocking the way she was moving her hands without any clubs to throw. Without breaking her focus or rhythm, she kicked out with her right foot and caught him on the shin, hearing a satisfying 'ouch!'.

Still, Kelly watched the hands. She had it now, though, and knew she didn't need to watch any more. She raised her eyes to Tom's and saw him wink at her. She smiled. And then, as though they had practised this a million times, Tom's rhythm changed slightly, and he flicked one club away from himself and towards Kelly. Without even thinking, she caught it and flicked it back to him. She might have been performing the catch-and-release all her life. Tom did it again, and she returned to the club without hesitation. She heard some muttering among the group of boys who had been trying to juggle. It didn't matter.

Tom flicked two clubs towards her in quick succession, and she returned them in a blur, with no conscious thought. Part of her mind was telling her that this was the most amazing thing that had ever happened to her, that she had been waiting for this all her life. Another part was refusing to believe it was happening, but she could see with her own eyes, and she knew she was really doing it. Her mind sparkled like the rainbow clubs.

And now Tom stepped it up. The clubs were flying from him to Kelly and back again, and the rhythm was perfect. She responded to every slight adjustment, every change of pattern, she just knew how to do it. With a laugh, she flicked one of the clubs high in the air so that it came back to Tom at a different point in his pattern, and she heard him whistle his appreciation as he caught and released it into the rest of the tumbling rainbow.

Focus was everything. With no room for self-doubt and no awareness of anything except her hands and the rainbow, Kelly's world had simultaneously shrunk and expanded into infinity.

Tom and Kelly each took a step backwards at the same time, without breaking the flow. Tom had started to slow down a little and Kelly went with him.

The rhythm slowed more, and Kelly saw that Tom was withdrawing clubs from the pattern after every five or six catches. He had one under each arm now, but his movements were as smooth as ever. He looked at Kelly and raised an eyebrow. She got it. After her next five catches, she deftly retained the next club in her left hand and swung it round to grip it under her right arm. There were only three left now, and she caught the next one swiftly, tucking it under her left arm.

The last two clubs were in the air. Tom and Kelly caught one each at exactly the same moment, as though they had been working together all their lives, and, without thinking about it, turned towards the rest of the room, holding the clubs above their heads and waving with their free hands.

There was a moment of silence, and then the hall echoed with cheers and applause. Kelly looked out at her classmates and saw them all looking at her; seeing her. She smiled at Tom and said thank you quietly before turning towards the door.

As she walked out of the hall, Ryan caught up with her, dropping his arm around her shoulders and saying, "Hey Kelly, do you wanna…"

She turned to look at him, lifted his hand carefully and removed it from her shoulders.

"No." she said, "No, actually, I don't think I do."

11. The Real Fake News

Paul Barnett

I remember I became very depressed at the time. It was as if I were collapsing from the inside. If it hadn't been for my elderly neighbour, Alexi Orlov, I don't know what might have come of me. He was an inspiration to so many back then, although he would have been the first to deny it.

"We have no choice but to carry on, my dear," he would say, smiling, his face crinkling.

In a time of hunger and fear, it is not always easy to be noble, but Alexi found a way, no matter what the personal cost. I felt it my duty to show my support. So that on the day of his release, I went to the prison as the snow swirled about me, and the sky was the colour of turned meat in a butcher's window. A cold blast was lifting from the nearby river.

Iosif, one of Alexi's oldest friends, was already there, waiting. Others wanted to come, but the Party's faithful were forever watching, stoking fear on a daily basis.

Iosif greeted me, rubbing my arms to give me additional warmth.

"He'll be fine, Misha", he said, though he had no way of knowing that.

Finally, a small door opened in the corner of the large wooden gates and outstepped a shrunken version of the Alexi we both knew and loved. My breath clutched in my chest. He was as frail as a bubble, his skin a ghostly colour. But when he neared, he gave his familiar cracked, defiant smile and said, "Imagine if I wrote something they really didn't like."

I choked back tears as he put his arms around us.

"Ah, the beautiful Misha," Alexi said, turning to me. "You really shouldn't have come, my dear."

"Is it a crime to help a neighbour, now?"

"Don't give them ideas," he whispered theatrically.

We took the trolley bus home. It was humbling to me to see the smiles on the people who saw and recognised Alexi.

"Perhaps you should stay with me on the ground floor, Alexi", I said when we finally reached the apartment block where we both lived. I was certain the three flights of stairs up to his own apartment would kill him.

"No, no, my dear, I'll be fine," Alexi said, holding my hand. "Besides, I think your young man, Demetri, would have something to say about that, don't you?"

I looked away, ashamed. Demetri worked as a journalist on the only available newspaper, The Fox, a well-known propagandist rag created to lavish praise on our dear leader.

With considerable effort, we reached Alexi's front door just as he became convulsed in a fit of coughing, spitting blood into a rag. We settled him into his bed. Iosif set about making a fire in the hearth while I prepared a little vegetable broth.

I spoon-fed Alexi as he sat, propped up by a bank of pillows, surrounded by candles mashed into saucers. Despite our insistence he rest, Alexi bombarded us with questions. We told him of the latest audacities of the President, a man who had seized power with promises of making the country great again. That greatness was reserved for a precious few, others like him who put personal wealth over decency. The rest of us were left scavenging in the dirt for the pickings.

I didn't like leaving Alexi that first night. Dying alone is a personal dread of my own, but he shooed us away with a smile and a wave of his hand.

"Go, go, and give an old man a little peace."

Iosif walked me back down the stairwell, in silence. He said goodbye at my door with a shake of his head as if everything had a poorly scripted inevitability about it. I watched him make his way across the square, collar pulled up against the now-driving snow. A white canvas was stretched between the apartment blocks, under the yellow glare of streetlights.

I took a deep breath before opening the door to my one-room apartment. Demetri was sat near the window in almost darkness, drinking, his mood obvious.

"Don't lecture me, Demetri," I said, "I'm too tired to fight; you'll only wake Anna."

Demetri nodded insincerely and, in a measured voice, said, "'Good that you think of Anna, Misha. Will you think of her still when they rip her from your arms because they most certainly will?"'

"You're being overly dramatic."

"Am I? You know how this reflects on me."

Ignoring him, I started to undress next to the bed. In a forced whisper, Demetri said, "I could beat you; some husbands would, you know."

Without turning to face him, I folded my clothes and said, "Then, I would love you less than I already do."

***

Before the new regime had seized power, I had notions of a doctorate in chemistry, but they found other uses for my talents. Instead, they had me work as a cleaner at the offices of the Ministry of Transportation. It was another example of their cruel humour, especially as the people were not allowed to travel freely. Everywhere you looked, there were faces of hunger and want.

My supervisor, a detestable Armenian by the name of Hirat, was a part-time pimp and one-time pig farmer. He had prospered as a member of the Party faithful, proof that scum always floats. The brothel he ran was in the basement of the Ministry of Transportation and, therefore, effectively state sponsored.

"I hear the cripple is home," Hirat said as I mopped the floor in large sweeping arches. His gold tooth flashed, and his breath smelt of whisky and herring. "They say he does not have long."

I had schooled myself not to react.

"Remember to pick your friends wisely, Misha," he said as he walked away, "I would hate to see that pretty face of yours working in the basement."

His laugh sent a wave of revulsion through me. He made me wonder about the life he and his kind lived inside, one devoid of moral decency and principles, one that was self-serving and filled with prejudice; bastards, every one of them.

In the weeks that followed, some of Alexi's friends would visit; the authors and artists who were no longer published could no longer exhibit their work. Although he spent most of his days dozing, Alexi would animate in their company. Sometimes, he would ask them to read to him from The Fox.

"Why; you know how angry that partisan rubbish makes you," his friends would say.

"So, when you leave, I can use it to wipe my ass," Alexi would chuckle, shooting me an apologetic smile.

***

When word got out that I was nursing Alexi, I was ushered to the front of food lines. Butchers and grocers made a point of slipping me extra provisions beyond my ration entitlement. But the more I cared for Alexi, the more Demetri's mood darkened, and his drinking increased. Once he tried to stop me leaving the apartment, standing between me and the door.

"You cannot fight fate," he said in a forced whisper, with Anna playing on the floor near us.

"That doesn't mean I have to embrace it like you," I hissed.

We were locked in a levelling look before I said, "You more than anyone should know what is happening here, Demetri. What has happened to you?"

I pushed past and made my way up the stairs as he called after me," I accepted my responsibilities, and so should you, Misha."

Demetri and Alexi were alike in one respect; neither one gave way to self-pity. But where Alexi still had fight, Demetri appeared to simply adjust his soul to the prevailing conditions, and a part of me hated him for that.

We began to pass one another like ghosts in our single, one-room apartment. At night, our bed was as cold as the tundra.

My love for Alexi and his work increased. I felt emboldened to find small ways of my own to challenge the Party. I attended block meetings and asked awkward questions of local officials who were used to the theatre of listening to the people's complaints. I asked about missing journalists, about the fake news the Party was pushing.

Attendance at these meetings increased. On one occasion, two large, heavyset men in expensive suits with menacing looks appeared. One sat near me, stabbing me with his smile as he took his seat.

Halfway through the meeting, I stood up brandishing a copy of Defiant, a flyer that had been doing the rounds in the precincts. It spoke of the corruption in government and how leading party officials were living a life of luxury while the people starved. The local party representatives blustered when I confronted them with the allegations Defiant had made.

The heavyset man nodded when I sat back down. There was even a smattering of applause. The officials told us they would have answers to my questions at the next meeting, which everyone knew was a lie.

After the meeting, people came up to talk to me on the snowy steps outside. There was talk of organising ourselves, of holding meetings of our own. It wasn't prudent to be seen as a group for long, so we scattered, promising to meet again.

Walking home, I wrapped my coat tightly around me and noticed the heavyset man, off at a distance, with his friend, smoking. He put his hand up and waved. I nodded and walked a little faster, only to hear them falling into step, on the crisp white snow behind me.

"Wait," one said when they had gained ground on me.

I glanced back and was shocked to see how close they were. "I must get home for my daughter," I said, hoping to appeal to any sense of decency they may have. My heart beat faster as they raced to catch up.

"Wait," the man who had sat next to me said again, grabbing my arm and turning me around. Facing them, I attempted to control my breath so as not to give in to the panic that was threatening to envelop me.

"Please," I said.

"We just think you made some valid points back there," the other, giant of a man, said. "What is it you want?"

I wasn't sure I understood him. "What do you mean?"

"From your outbursts at these meetings, what is it you want?"

I stalled, wondering if they might be allies. "An end to the injustice and cruelty. It's what we all want."

The first man nodded and said: "You don't think the Party has the people's interest at heart?"

"No," I blurted on a wave of courage.

They looked at one another and smiled. I flinched when the first man reached up and ran the back of a finger down my cheek and said, "'Well, you're wrong. The Party listens to all its people. If you are listening correctly, you will know you already have the answers to all your questions, and you will stop asking them. Do we understand one another, Misha?"'

I was still shaking with fear when I got in that night.

**

The rage I felt at what was happening all around me came. I took out on Demetri. I blamed his compliance, his cowardice and the propagandist bile he wrote for everything. Repeatedly I told him he wasn't a man if he could not stand up for what he thought was right. Sometimes our fighting became so rabid it tipped towards violence on both sides. Then we just stopped talking altogether.

One evening, I went into Alexi's apartment only to find him collapsed on the floor, gasping for air. I was too weak and drained to lift him on my own. In a blind panic, I raced downstairs to fetch Demetri. Thankfully, he reacted without rancour.

In the short time I had been away, Alexi's condition had worsened, and it was clear he did not have long. Demetri lifted him up and gently placed him onto the bed. Alexi gave a weak smile when he focused on Demetri. Patting his arm, he said: "At last we meet. You will find everything you need under the floorboards under the stove in the kitchen. Good luck, my boy."

Demetri nodded just as Alexi took his final breath. The air in the room tightened. I sobbed quietly, holding Alexi's hand.

Demetri came over to my side of the bed. He put his hand on my shoulder and said, "Go home, Misha; take care of Anna. I will do what needs to be done here."

I was overcome with grief and too exhausted to do anything more.

From my own apartment, I watched, blankly, as the night began to slowly opaque outside. Candles started to appear in the windows, in open defiance of the Party, and out of respect for Alexi.

A tap at the door startled me.

"Who is it?" I asked, rocking Anna in my arms.

"It's me, Misha. Quickly, quickly open up."

Demetri came barrelling in with a box of books and papers.

"What is that?"

"Alexi's scandal on the Party."

I watched as he started looking for places to hide the papers. A few he placed on the table alongside his old sit-up typewrite.

"What are you doing? And what was all that with, Alexi?"

Sitting at his typewriter, he ignored me and began working.

"Demetri, speak to me."

Without looking up, he took a deep breath and said, "I'm writing Alexi's obituary, the truth the people need to hear."

"But they won't let you publish it. Demetri, what is going on?"

He carried on, organising his desk, loading paper into his typewriter. "Who do you think is the author behind that flyer you're always talking about, Defiant?"

The shock hit me in a wave. "You?!"

He nodded, returning the carriage to his typewriter.

"But why didn't you say something?"

"I thought it safer, but you didn't know. You almost ruined everything by bringing the Party to our door."

I just stared at him as he wrote, attempting to process everything. It was a moment before I could go to him. Draping my arm around his shoulder, I kissed him on the corner of his mouth and said, "Don't be long before coming to bed. It's late."

He nodded without looking at me.

I got changed for bed and pulled the covers over to a sweet lullaby of tap, tap, tapping as the tundra beneath me began to melt.

12. Happy New Year

Millie Capon

Cities may always seem to be alive, but New Year's Eve in New York City has a particular spark. It is lit up with anticipation and illuminated by the truths of the thousands that gather. Behind each imperfect person is their imperfect story, but amidst it all, there is love at the centre.

Cheerful cries of excitement could be heard above the noise of skates around the outside of the Wollman Ice Rink in Central Park. There was a chill hanging in the air, but spectators stood about, wrapped tightly in coats, cupping hot chocolates in both hands. Amongst the many, a family of four stood patiently in the queue to hire ice skates for a few hours of unbridled joy. The eight-year-old twins were dressed head to toe in matching outfits: white tights, pink sweaters, denim dungaree dresses and cream puffer jackets. They held each other's hands tightly, woolly mittens keeping them warm. Tianna wore her black hair tightly in box braids beneath a bobble hat, while Amelie allowed the curls to bounce free – too thick for a hat to fit over but thick enough to keep her head warm. Luke and Rebecca stood behind the twins, clutching their worn-out skates, Luke's pale hand resting around Rebecca's waist. They chattered between themselves as the queue moved forward, the twins excited and filled with adoration for their foster parents.

As they reached the shack for the ice skate hire, the twins took off their boots and stood on tiptoes to hand them through the hatch. Moving down the line, they received identical pairs of skates and ran off to the rows of benches to put them on. Luke and Rebecca helped them before popping on their own skates.

A voice announced over the speaker that the late afternoon skate session was about to begin, and the twins leapt up from the bench and walked over to the rink. Luke leant over to Rebecca, a look of pride in his eyes, before closing them to kiss his wife on the cheek. They got up together and went to be with the girls, ready to introduce them to Taylor family traditions to break in the new year.

Their first steps onto the ice were hesitant, but there was such a joy in what they were doing for the first time. The initial loops around the rink were slow and a little wobbly, but they never let each other go, and Amelie held tight to the wall as they scooted round. Luke and Rebecca were experienced on the ice but held back to take photos of the girls and to provide encouraging words as they got a little braver.

They began to steady themselves and gained momentum. As their confidence grew, they let go of each other, though never left one another's side. Rebecca left them for a while, skating faster and nearer the inside edge of the outer skating ring. Her knees were slightly bent, and she was leaning forward. She moved fluidly and with grace. She was sure of the ice and at home in her skates. Luke and Rebecca tag-teamed, taking it in turns to skate closely behind the twins before skating off at speed in the centre.

Light snowflakes started to fall from the sky. There was an energy on the rink and an excitement off the ice. Passers-by would watch as they walked and talked, large groups of people passing through to Fifth Avenue en route to Times Square – a flash of orange getting lost amongst them as a lady walked quickly within the crowds.

At the heart of Manhattan, Central Park lies amongst the chaos. Parts seem dormant and peacefully still while the everyday comings and goings still make their way through. The trees root deep there, and the roots hold the secrets of the people who walk above them. Individuals exchange polite greetings, creating chosen family amongst strangers. The constant stream of people contributes to the innate sense of rhythm, a community that is ever-changing. They come to rest within the ebb and flow, each person finding their place there – the perfect haven for artists, athletes, schemers and daydreamers, musicians, magicians, and every type of soul you could imagine inhabiting the streets.

On this particular evening, a lady wandered through, her mind miles away. The last of the afternoon sun glowed through the naked tree branches. Tanya strolled, thigh-high black boots audible from a distance and orange coat swooshing as she walked steadily, but her hazel eyes dared not look up from the ground. Her black satchel swung, hanging from her left shoulder.

Eventually, she paused and took a seat on a bench next to a holly tree. She often paused here as it was a part of the park that felt still.

Holly trees grow gradually, so while New York continues to move at speed, the bush grows at a pace rarely seen in the city. The lady pulled a journal and Parker pen from the satchel and opened up the small book. Lying within the inside cover, there was a photo of a boy, her son. When her husband died suddenly seven years ago, Tanya couldn't seem to connect with him in the same way. The pair became distant as he set about working towards a career in music, and they were no longer in touch. Tanya let out a gentle sigh, a breeze passed through, and it was like the trees sighed with her. The wind passed through with a sense of balance, with a wisdom to move through steadily without the need to rush. Tanya looked at the photo a while before turning to a fresh page.

She began writing with a restless hand, a letter that she would never send to her son, as she did every New Year's Eve. She would write reflections from the year past, narrating her thoughts and feelings while posing questions to Joshua. She wondered where he found himself this New Year's Eve.

A young man ambled into the park that same early evening. He was tall and slender, wearing pale blue jeans, an oversized grey sweater, and a black duffle coat. He carried his guitar case in his left hand before settling by Bethesda Fountain. Having stopped, he pulled out his guitar – the same one he had owned since he was sixteen – and pushed the open case to face the pavement in front of him. As he stood, his mop of unruly brown hair fell in front of his face. He flicked it away, revealing his green flecks of his eyes glowing in the low light of the evening. Josh put his hand into his pocket and candidly tossed out the loose change that he had found. He tucked the microphone stand just behind the case and tested a 'one, two' into it while pushing his Clark Kent glasses up the bridge of his nose. Adjusting the red amp to his right, he fiddled for a while before plugging in a lead and placing the guitar strap around his neck.

He breathed in deeply before strumming a single chord – as if to announce that he was ready to begin.

Passers-by continued to stroll and chatter amongst themselves with the buzz of New Year's Eve on their lips as they made their way to Time Square. Josh was filled with a nervous energy that he couldn't quite explain and began to play.

Tanya could hear the music from a distance and listened intently, lifting her head from her journal. The voice sounded familiar to her, and her restless heart began to beat ever faster. She could not place the sound on the timeline of her past.

Where Josh played, some people stopped around the fountain and listened a while. Others listened but carried on their way. Some were so absorbed in their own thoughts that anything beyond that was unreachable. A song or two in, Josh took a deep breath and said, "Another year passes, but even now, I think of you."

He began to finger-pick a simple melody on his guitar before singing out with every inch of breath in his lungs like he was calling out into the park. Each note he sang sounded like it was inscribed in his heart, and it reached beyond being notes on a stave, becoming music in motion with emotion. The chords rang out and passed through Tanya's body, taking her back to sitting amongst hundreds in the school hall, listening to her boy play. She put down her pen – the pain of long-ago memories aching in her body, so she decided to continue her way – shutting off her heart's yearning so she couldn't feel the pain. She got to her feet and hurriedly put the journal back in her satchel as she walked.

Joshua's voice continued to surround her, but the words seemed to muffle together – never quite reaching her.

Passing Joshua by, she looked up briefly, peering round the orange of her coat collar, only to catch his eye for a second before looking down at the pavement again. The song ended. Time seemed to stand still but rushed through all at once. The music rang out. It could almost have been a movie scene had she not proceeded onwards and out of Central Park.

Josh paused, replaying the orange blur over and over, his hazel eyes wide, wild and youthful. His heart sounded beneath his sweater, and he was left wondering if that really could have been her.

The High Line hovers above the hustle and bustle. People find themselves there to get a view of Manhattan, to find perspective, and to find a new dream or two; it seems to breathe new life into all those who wander lost. Sammy found himself out on a walk this New Year's Eve. He ambled a while before coming to sit amongst the foliage on a bench, resting his white cane to his right. Streetlights illuminated the busyness below, the High Line a safe vantage point to be a part of, yet apart from the chaos beneath. Soft orange hues glowed from the windows of apartment blocks while the lights of the city shone loud and bright. The scene was alive with the echoes of shared experiences, moved by groups of family and friends and strangers alike.

Though alone, Sammy wasn't lonely. Mind busy but heart still and in awe of all that he could hear, his mind's eye built the picture for him. At the very edge of his darkness, light could make its way into vision.

Sammy took the red Beats headphones resting around his neck and placed them over his head, the blaring music from them rising above the noise of New York City. The wind moved through every now and again at speed, so he pulled the sleeves of his green hoodie over his hands, clutching the fabric in both palms.

A snow flurry began, and he relaxed his head back to look up towards the sky. As he breathed deeply, his breath was visible in the air. The aromas of crowded street stalls rose up to him, and his mouth watered. Taking his cane in hand, he removed his headphones as he got to his feet and made his way along the High Line towards a stand selling hot dogs, just the way he liked them, with plenty of mustard. A young woman stood alongside him while they waited to be served. She wore a plain white tee tucked into high-waisted black jeans with ankle boots. Her coat was pale blue and fleecy to touch.

Sammy could smell her perfume above the greasy food – distinctively London's Jo Malone Nutmeg and Ginger fragrance - not that he knew this. He just knew the smell of sophistication and that it was a scent he'd known before.

"Lovely evening out," Sammy uttered, slightly breathless.

"Lovely evening indeed," the lady replied, looking at him with eyes bright, her face kind. She smiled broadly at him; he could sense it. They stood making small talk for a while, both making their orders at the stand between introductions. Martha shuffled her weight from one foot to the other – nervous but completely enchanted.

"Who are you with this evening?" she asked, looking around beyond the gathering at the stand.

"No one, Ma'am, just me tonight." He responded, not an ounce of self-pity in his voice.

"May I stay?" she asked, "No one should find themselves alone on New Year's Eve. My friends are making their way to Times Square. We can walk here; the others will take the subway into the centre, but we can walk and talk along the High Line a while if you like?"

"I'd like that," he answered. Martha waved a small group of people away in the distance, and they continued to walk on, followed by a lady in an orange coat walking hastily who overtook them. The group noticed her but thought little of her upset, though it was unusual to see someone alone in the hours before midnight.

The pair collected their hotdogs. She liked hers plain. Martha chuckled as he spilt mustard down his chin and reached out to wipe it away with her thumb. Her hands were soft but chilly. Sammy felt safe with her; she spoke softly but seemed confident enough for the both of them. When they'd finished standing around eating, he reached out, put her hands into his and held them up to his mouth, breathing gently into the clasp of hands. His breath warmed them through before they walked hand in hand into the night. They walked steadily; casual chatter became a conversation of the year gone by and the year ahead, the perfect night to meet someone and have plenty to talk about.

The countdown to midnight had moments to go. Though it was late, people filed in and out of the shops. It got busier as midnight neared, and the square became crowded.

People loitered around with half pints in hand, looking up towards the bright lights. Amongst the thousands stood stories written by the people of New York City, moments in time captured by those who gathered. Laughter bubbled up like champagne.

A lady stood on the outskirts, wrapped tightly in her orange coat. Tanya felt distant from the surrounding noise, her ears hearing only her heartbeat and the sound of her son's voice. She felt close to him, though they were apart. He was lost in the crowd.

Luke and Rebecca held the twins close to them, huddling for warmth. Their individual heartbeats pulsed as one.

Martha stood by Sammy's side on the High Line, looking out - describing all that could be seen. Every now and again, he'd add details of what he was imagining into the scene, and together, they built a beautiful picture of Manhattan. The countdown began, "five, four, three, two, one," and with that, a new year sounded in to the untuned bangs of fireworks.

13. Cinderella
(The True Story as Recounted by Her Stepsister to our Royal Correspondent)

Jude Painter

There has been much fake news and some alternative facts about Princess Ella's early home life and the time she spent in our house, much of it unfavourable to my sister and myself, so that I welcome the opportunity to set matters straight.

Ella and her father moved in with my sister, mother and myself after the death of her own mother, his wife, when, after quite a short time, he married our mother. When they came to us, we could immediately see that they were both very needy, and we opened our hearts to them. He is a man who chooses to remain alone in his study at all times, practising his cornet, cataloguing his collection, and eating Jammy Dodgers. He is not at all concerned about his daughter or his new stepdaughters.

Fortunately, my sister and I are close to our own dear mama, a remarkable woman. She spends nearly all her time sitting up in her bed, taking an active interest in the television programmes she watches, responding to them by shouting. My sister is a large woman, hirsute and well-endowed, with a rosy complexion and a loud, even at times quite a booming voice. I do not wish to describe myself except to say that I am always at the forefront of the latest fashions. My legs are probably my most impressive feature and have frequently been known to elicit gasps of amazement when I enter a room. But enough about us, I have promised to give my view of the period the princess, then just plain Ella, was with us.

She tended to wear shabby grey and dusty black clothes all the time, which quite frankly did nothing for her pale complexion. My sister and I both favour a colourful wardrobe, so you can imagine we created so much of a contrast with her that when visitors came, it was thought best for little Ella to remain behind the scenes, sweeping the chimneys or taming the billy goat; her therapeutic work.

I first began to fear that she had issues when I entered the kitchen one day to check on her and found her holding a necessarily one-sided conversation with a couple of mice and a rat. Apart from her relationship with rodents, she also entertained a visitor who would appear at the most unexpected times in a variety of glitzy, sparkling costumes and declaim in rhyming couplets. This ethereal female was doubtless seen by the girl as a kind of 'mother figure', surely some sort of surrogate for her own dead mother.

We knew she would not be happy having a huge bedchamber like the rest of the family, so she curled up in the nice warm kitchen beside the fire at night with the cat which was convenient for breadmaking and other early morning duties.

One day a gold embossed letter arrived inviting our household to attend the prince's ball, an annual event held for the great and good (and many celebrities). Ella got it into her head that she wanted to go. I, being the most sensitive of her stepsisters could immediately imagine poor naive Ella getting mixed up with faded has-beens from I'm a Celebrity, Get Me Out of Here, journalists and other undesirables. With her fragile mental state, I could just picture the sort of trouble she might get into. I pointed out to her that she would be safer at home and would not be bored as she had a pig to kill, gut and marinate for Sunday…more therapeutic work to stop her brooding.

The foolish child found a way to attend the ball but returned home after midnight in a state of despair and dishevelment, shoeless and in her habitual rags. We did not like to enquire what had happened.

You will doubtless have heard and read some bewildering reports about the glass slipper incident. On the following day, the prince came around to our house. It appears that at the ball, he had hit it off with a woman he danced with and fancied himself in love with. He can remember little about her (the drink, I expect) except that she was wearing glass slippers, one of which she left behind in her haste to leave. To me, this story has a hint of fantasy about it. For example, I ask you: - has any man ever noticed anything the woman he loves is wearing, especially her footwear?

Anyway, he and his enormous retinue entered our home with the shoe on a cushion, saying that whoever it fitted should be his wife. There was a great deal of media interest in the story, and he was accompanied by reporters and at least one television crew. The visit threw the household into an uproar. Dear Mama was ensconced in her bed in the bathroom watching a documentary about the rainforest with David Attenborough, one of her favourites. In her haste to change out of her tropical gear to go and meet real-live royalty, she became entangled in her mosquito net and required the attention of the whole household in order to be extricated. For once, father appeared, beard covered in the usual fine sprinkling of J D crumbs. He was anxious to show his collection of unusually shaped vegetables to our royal visitor. It took the combined efforts of all of us to dissuade him.

I brought out one of my prettier clogs to try to tempt this man, who I would not for a moment accuse of having such a serious condition as a shoe fetish, certainly showed what can only be described as an unusual interest in women's footwear. I must add that at that time, I had reason to believe I might be the lady the prince had become infatuated with as we had enjoyed a dance together at the ball. When it was over, he admittedly, rather breathless and green-faced, had complimented me on my dancing. He said he had never been lifted so high or spun around so fast in his entire life. However, he was adamant that the woman he had fallen in love with had been the glass slipper wearer and only the owner of the foot which it fitted could be the woman he would marry.

So, my sister (a size eleven and a half, forty-five continental, if ever I saw one!) tried to squeeze her feet into tight socks in order to reduce the size of her feet while I decided that a glass slipper constituted a serious health and safety hazard. At any rate, by this time, I was not at all convinced I could be happy with a man who wore pale blue satin trousers in the daytime, even if he was a prince, and did not attempt to try the shoe on.

At that moment, Ella wandered into the kitchen carrying a bucket of coal and a sack of logs, singing to herself. The prince, in a spirit of providing equality of opportunity for all (he was being filmed at the time), decreed she should also try the glass slipper. It fitted, and both he and Cinderella were overjoyed.

It took some time to cut my sister free of the tight socks and to persuade father to take his obscene vegetables back to his room. Our mother was justifiably disappointed that neither of her own daughters had captured the heart of the prince, went back to her bed happily thinking of plans she and one of the television people had been discussing for a reality television series based on our family.

We realised that Ella's removal to the palace would mean a great deal of inconvenience to the household but reassured ourselves that with our help, she had now been able to resolve her issues and move forward.

On behalf of my sister and myself, I offer congratulations to the happy couple. I sincerely hope Princess Ella and Prince Charming will be deeply happy. Doubtless, they will be as they are obviously well suited, with her penchant for conversing with rodents, and I suspect he is one of those princes who talks to plants.

14. The Theory of Nothing

Paul Barnett

Light slats into the room from the small window with its shatterproof glass. The desk and chair are bolted to the floor. The pictures are bolted to the walls. There's a wall that separates the toilet from the rest of the room, but there's no door.

For a very long time, too long maybe Marty had been of the opinion that most days are unremarkable. Yesterday had been different, for sure. It had landed him here, for one thing.

Sitting on the edge of his bunk, Marty smiles. Even in this stark room, he finds a vibrating energy he has never experienced before. He wonders if the feeling will fade, but he intuits that it won't, though the intensity may vary. He has crossed a line and can't unlearn what he now holds to be true. He no longer has one single idea about himself, not one, and he's never been so happy or content.

There's a noise outside his door, then a gentle tap. The lock is opened, and a younger woman, whom Marty vaguely remembers from last night, enters. She looks surprised to see him sat up and dressed.

"Are you okay?" she says, in a Bristolian accent.

Marty wonders if that's a trick question, given where he is. Marty nods, smiles. He can't help smiling now. It's as if his facial features have found a new way to naturally configure.

"Have you not slept at all?"

Marty shakes his head: "Not really."

"You should be still out of it with what they pumped into you. I'm one of the nurses, by the way, Rachel, Rach."

"Pleased to meet you." Marty notes her casual dress, jeans and a hoodie, and her blonde hair is tied back in a ponytail.

"And you, Marty. Would you be up to seeing the psyche now?"

Marty nods. He's never seen a psyche before. He wonders if there will be talk of egos and ids. He wonders what a psyche may make of what has happened.

Rach asks questions as they walk along the corridor.

"Any pain, discomfort?"

Marty shakes his head.

"Depression?"

"No, you?"

"Funny," Rach says, smiling.

"Thanks."

"No hallucinations, suicidal thoughts?"

Marty shakes his head.

"Why are you smiling?"

Marty shrugs.

"It's not a complaint. It's just not usual, least not with new admissions."

Rach says good morning to people they pass. They give Marty a look, and he wonders if they recognise him from last night's local news.

"I'll introduce you to everyone later."

Marty nods.

They climb a dogleg staircase up to another floor. Rach asks him to take a seat outside the office she enters.

Marty breathes deeply and contentedly. He notices that his knee isn't bouncing with his usual excess nervous energy. Ordinarily, his anxieties would have been off the chart coming to a place like this. In the past, he'd do anything to mask those anxieties, to keep them hidden from the world. In a crowd, he'd go out of his way to win the room, to be seen as the funniest, the smartest, always talking, always joking.

Now, he feels he could be set down in just about any place on earth, and he'd be perfectly fine. He's found a comfort in quiet that he has never experienced before. When you get right down to it, was there that much worth saying anyway?

"You can go in. Dr Powel will see you now," Rach says, smiling, holding the door open for him.

There's no couch as Marty was expecting, just two large, comfy-looking chairs facing each other over by the window. A woman is sat in one with a notepad and a pen. In conceptual time, Marty would say she was in her fifties, but what did that even mean now? If life and death were an illusion, then surely time must be also.

"Take a seat, Marty," she says, smiling and giving a little nod to the other chair. She looks at him as if she is searching for something. Marty smiles.

"How're you feeling?"

"Good."

"Do you know where you are, Marty?"

"Willow Lodge; an assessment unit for those considered to be a risk to themselves or others."

"Very good, and do you know why you're here?"

"I straddled the barrier on the suspension bridge and threatened to jump."

Dr Powel nods and says, "You did. Do you know why you did that?"

Marty looks out the window to the lovingly tended gardens below. The liveliness of nature is almost overwhelming to him now. He looks back and says, "I suppose I'd been ripe for suicide for a long time. Like most people, I'd been propelled by a talent for optimism, always hoping for a better version of myself. Then I started waking up to the fact it was never going to happen. You see, doctor, we start out busy, so we don't have to see how futile the running is. Everything we do is just silly because we all die in the end."

"You were out on that ledge for a while. Was there a significant event that triggered you doing what you did?"

Marty tried pinning something down but couldn't come up with anything. "I hadn't been sleeping."

"And what would you do when you couldn't sleep?"

"Well, I'd read into the early hours, but then I'd get to a point where I couldn't read. The words on the page would turn into tiny little spiders and scuttle off the page."

"Spiders?"

Marty smiles at her, taking him literally: "I just mean the words would blur in my exhaustion. I didn't actually see spiders."

"Did you ever self-medicate?"

"Alcohol?"

"Or drugs."

"Yes, to both."

"Were you high when you crawled over the barrier, Marty?"

Marty shook his head.

"Can you describe what was going through your mind at the time?"

Marty hesitates. He feels that what he wants to say can't be adequately conveyed in words because it can't be understood totally by the intellect alone. It is more experiential. He smiles, realising he is in the right place for sounding crazy. "I felt I couldn't live with myself, that I hated myself."

"Okay," Dr Powel says, leaning back, making notes.

"But then I started to ponder the question: How can I hate myself? That would imply there are two of me. There's the one hated and the one doing the hating. As you can see, there isn't two of me. Isn't that curious?"

Dr Powel smiles. "Isn't it just an expression?"

"But it got me thinking."

"And what did you come up with, Marty?"

Marty takes a moment to look around. He nods to pictures on Dr Powel's desk, presumably of her family. "Do you like going to the pictures, the cinema, Dr Powel?"

Momentarily thrown by the question, Dr Powel says, yes, she does.

"Well, when we go to the cinema, we identify with the characters we see up on the screen."

"Go on."

"But the following week, there is a new film and new characters up on the same screen, yet somehow it doesn't ruin the illusion for us; isn't that, right?"

"Yes, I can see that."

"Supposing instead of identifying with the characters on the screen, which are always coming and going and changing, we saw ourselves as the screen? The screen is always the same, every week, always consistent; everything that comes afterwards is just mere projection."

Dr Powel pulls a face and says, "Are you saying you had some religious or spiritual epiphany, Marty?"

"I'd say that religion is just more labels, not always helpful labels either. As a species, we've a fondness for labels." Marty leans in like he is conspiring, "A tiger doesn't know it's a tiger. It's only because we call it a tiger. It doesn't go around the jungle bragging it's a tiger if you get me, Dr Powel."

Dr Powel smiles, making notes: "So what shall we call it, this insight you say you had?"

"Let's break with tradition and not call it anything, or maybe nothing for now."

"So out on the bridge, you suddenly felt, um, nothing."

"Pretty much, yes. We're all the same under the masks we wear, you see. The person one grows into is the character on the screen, the actor in the film. When all along, the empty screen underneath might be who we truly are."

"And for you, the mask fell away?"

"I was at my lowest point, out on the bridge, and maybe that's what it took for the mask to fall away. In that second, I felt a sudden absence of everything, my past achievements and failures, future ambitions, viewpoints. All the labels had gone. Identification with everything just slipped away. What was left was, well, emptiness, a pure and simple nothingness, and yet it is everything at the same time. It probably doesn't make sense, and I'm not sure it is even meant to."

Dr Powel takes notes.

"You see, we're all so busy grasping at things we think will make us happy we don't realise the lesson the universe is trying to teach us all the time."

"Which is?"

"To just let go."

Dr Powel smiles. "Maybe we could try something else. Tell me about your work?"

"What about it?

"You're a PhD student at the university, physics, quantum mechanics, is that correct?"

"First year, yes."

"Must be quite a demanding course."

Marty smiles. "You're thinking my mind might have snapped?"

"It happens. But how do you reconcile this new understanding of yours with your interest in science? Isn't there some sort of conflict there? Where is the scientific rigour?"

Marty looks out the window at the poplar trees just swaying in the Autumn breeze. "All matter at its smallest component is just vibrating waves of energy. Everything in existence is fundamentally empty, devoid of an inherent self. And yet, all matter emits ripples of energy, like when you drop a pebble into a pond, the ripples go outwards."

"So why don't we know this?

"Because we can only perceive the world through the limited filter of our senses. We sense we are separated from everything and everyone else."

"So, if I have this correctly, you're saying that is wrong, and we're connected to everything?"

"In a way, yes. At least by our waves of energy. You can observe it in crowds and audiences, even in war zones. We tap into a shared energy, a shared emotion, sometimes good, sometimes bad, and then it spreads."

"That's quite a bold claim without experimentation to back it up."

Marty shrugs. "Maybe some things defy an equation. It would be difficult to measure love, yet we all seem to have a sense that it exists. Our interconnectedness makes all wars and conflicts futile. Effectively, we're just arguing with ourselves."

"And that's what you felt happened sat on the bridge; you acquired the ability to understand all this?"

"I didn't acquire anything. How can I acquire something I had all along, we all have? We just don't know we have it. Constantly identifying with the image on the screen prevents us from seeing the screen, our true selves. It gets in the way. It's like being poor your entire life only to find you had a diamond in your pocket all along."

"How does it feel, this shift in understanding?"

"A liberation."

Dr Powel smiles, nods, then looks at her watch: "Look, I hadn't planned to see you now, Marty and I have another appointment. If it's okay with you, I'd like you to remain with us just for the observation and assessment period of 28 days. We need to establish if what you're feeling is temporary and subject to change. Are you okay with that, Marty?"

Marty nods, smiles.

Dr Powel gets up and goes to the door: "Anyway, I'd be interested to learn more of this, um, theory of yours."

Leaving Marty says, "The Theory of Nothing, maybe?"

15. A Day in the Life of the Seasons

Millie Capon

Winter

With gentle whispers, Winter breathes life into The New Forest. Snowflakes tumble through the breaks in the forest ceiling to form one unbroken layer of snow upon the ground. The trees remain steadfast against each seasonal gust that passes through - perfectly poised like ballet dancers in 'The Nutcracker'. Each Oak tree branch is naked from Winter's grasp upon it but perfectly formed and laced with flakes of white. A spritely robin hops between the branches while looking about inquisitively – the snow confusing to him as he tries to seek out an opportunity for an easy meal.

Winter is an open invitation for childlike joy. As afternoon falls upon the forest, the woodland rouses to the sound of laughter. Amongst the many that gather there, a group of young adults ramble through in assorted woolly accessories, having arrived for a short holiday on the local campsite. They begin throwing snowballs at each other, tittering as they run ahead in various directions to avoid being the target of the next snowball. Two women walk slightly behind the group, keen to get a few moments alone, tentatively holding hands. A friend ahead turns around, and they quickly let go of each other, looking bashful.

Elsa and Sarah hold back and call out that they will 'catch the others up'. They stand closely to each other, giggling a little, looking up at the snow falling down. A tiny snowflake lands on Elsa's nose, and Sarah reaches out to touch it. Her right hand shakes a little, and she then goes to cup Elsa's cheek in her hand. Their eyes meet, and the rest of the world appears to melt away. Their lips quiver in the cold air but find warmth on each other's lips, sharing one breath.

Winter witnesses the innocence of this intimate moment and joyously shares in it with them as they hurry after their friends with their pinkie fingers linked together.

Spring

The playful touch of Spring brings a youthful spirit to the forest as Winter fades away. The trees stand grandly like an opera, and the sunlight conducts the forest as, together, they call forth the fresh season. Oak arms that were once exposed now bear an array of bright green foliage that creates a chromatogram of colour across the forestry.

Despite a coolness in the air, the promise of warmth stirs within. A plentiful time is coming, and the abundance creates a wild energy that fills the air. One can measure the depth of the morning by the presence of light and the company of dew upon the grass. The forest floor is bathed in sunlight, and the dewy droplets glisten. The dewdrops cling to individual strands of lawn; the first gift of many to the forest upon a new day. Bluebell roots absorb the gift, and the bright bonnets open out. From the burrows, tiny pink noses emerge, followed by white bodies that hop between the tree stumps. The rabbits bound from burrow to burrow, pausing only to munch upon dandelions. There is something about the way that they move, a delight, as they relish in the seasons changing.

A mother and her son ride their bikes along the path, their breath now quite invisible. He rides slightly ahead of her, seemingly a little unbalanced but still riding with a quiet confidence. His mother smiles, her sparkly eyes bursting with pride as he peddles off into the forestry. The boy lifts himself up from the saddle, grinning as he stands and peddles simultaneously, fast approaching a lake deeper within the forest.

Having taken a moment to look back, the boy soon realises that his mother isn't following behind him as closely as he thought, so he slows down to pull over on the side of the path. Eventually, his mother catches up to him and clambers off of her bike. Slightly breathless, she leans on a sturdy-looking tree and takes small sips from her water bottle. The boy's face wavers with a look of concern quickly covered over with a broad smile as his mother pulls a face at him.

From her rucksack, his mother pulls out a box of stale bread, and they go to the edge of the lake. The ducks gather in front of them as they throw small pieces of bread into the water. Once the bread is gone, the mother puts her arm round the boy's bony shoulders and places her chin on his head as they embrace. Tears gather in her eyes, but she blinks them back. She holds a hand to her stomach, the ache of loss catching her unaware. The boy backs away to look at his mother before stepping in close to her, clutching his hands around hers on her tummy. No words are shared between them, but there is an acknowledgement of the shared loss of the life that was and will always be.

Just past the tree, a patch of daffodils is in bloom. The mother plucks a few and wanders back to the water's edge, giving one to her son, Ben. Hand in hand, they throw their flowers into the water and watch the ripples spread across the pond. Grief amongst the abundance of new life breaks the heart of Spring. Despite their heavy hearts, a subtle warmth lingers; a soft glow from the sun attempts to lift the heartbreak felt. Lambs bleat in a nearby field – breaking the silence -- and drip, drip drops of April showers soon ring in, too. The pair return to their bikes as the rain begins to fall a little harder through the forest ceiling as if empathising with the loss in this season. The bluebell bonnets catch the raindrops and hang their heads as the weight becomes too much for their little bodies to bear.

Ben and his mother ride off together, side by side – his mother looking back briefly to see the daffodils floating on the lake in the distance. The smell of the woodland path becomes ever more present, a fresh earth scent growing stronger by the second. Ben chuckled as the rain fell harder -- lightness just inching in and his mother's gentle smile returning as he radiated.

Regardless of whether they were searching for it, the breath of Spring breathed a joyfulness into all those who found their way through the forest.

Summer

Though anticipated, Summer creeps in and arrives without much warning. The lake lays flat like a mirror, undisturbed, not a ripple in sight. With each passing moment, the lives of elders find themselves renewed. In the early morning of the longest day of the year, an older gent and his wife arrive, keen to absorb the arrival of Summer. They venture into the forest before the overwhelming humidity has the chance to rob them of the enjoyment of their outing.

The couple walk on the dried-out ground, not even a droplet of dew on the blades of grass round their ankles. The gentleman pauses, looks around him, and then strays off the path in search of a dandelion clock. He plucks one from the ground and blows gently, watching in awe as the seeds catch in the easy breeze and fly away upwards into the clearing. Though he does not know where they will land, he feels satisfied in the knowledge that they will plant themselves and begin their lifetime once more. Watching on, his wife, Betty, smiles, then comes alongside him and plucks one for herself. She takes a deep breath…and with each breath out, she counts forwards the hours. By the time she chants 'four o'clock', the stalk is empty, and the seeds are carried away in Summer's breath.

Arthur looks at his wife with adoration, remembering how, in Summer, they used to run through the dandelion clocks on a Friday after school with Bakewell tarts from the local bakery. Here they are, school sweethearts, fifty odd years later, enjoying the dandelions with the same joy, though with a little less youthful energy.

Summer has a funny way of allowing people in to reminisce of times that have passed, warming hearts and finding people where they are.

Autumn

It is around this time of year that the forest comes alive. As the October mornings arrive, Autumn is in full motion -- the golden glory of a year's end. Fruitful horse-chestnut and Oak trees stand surrounded by clusters of nuts thrown from them during a blustery night. Squirrels scamper across the forest floor, gathering supplies in anticipation of Winter. One, in particular, takes too many and drops them all before collecting them back together again.

A mild frost coats patches of moss, and wild mushrooms sit in pockets on every available surface. Sunlight peeps through, playful in the soft light; the colours pop like an abstract piece of art. Autumn gives by enlivening the senses crafting beautiful artistry from the changes.

A hazy mist hovers over the lake. Just months after their summer of dandelion clocks, Betty and Arthur walk around the lake, occasionally stopping to peer through their binoculars. Arthur gazes at his wife while she's busy spotting the birds, admiring her ageing skin and the way that her grey hair catches the light. At one point, Betty points out a single magpie, and in unison, they salute it, saying 'Good Morning, Mr Magpie,' and laugh a little.

Around lunchtime, they take a seat at a picnic bench. From the rucksack he was carrying, he pulls out a green coffee flask and some Tupperware boxes containing neatly wrapped sandwiches, two apples, mini cheddars and a Bakewell slice. They seem blissfully happy and as together as they ever had been.

The trees rustle in the breeze as leaves of every shape and colour fly wildly with each gust of wind, twisting and turning through the air. A family pull over to the left of the road, not far from the lake. The engine switches off, and the Johnson family sit silently for a moment. After a short while, Ben and his mother, alongside his father and sister, Katie, clamber out of the car. The kids begin clamouring about building 'the biggest den ever'. Katie wraps an old tartan red coat of her mother's tightly around her while Ben pulls on an oversized hand-me-down hoodie and navy wellington boots. The children's father takes his wife in his arms and hugs her gently, caressing her pregnant tummy with his fingertips. Leaves dance as they fall like confetti over the couple. The kids join the embrace before running on ahead into the seasonal wilderness, passing Betty and Arthur as they go.

Ben and Katie heap leaves up high. Once satisfied that the pile is big enough, Katie jumps into them. If it wasn't for her long, blonde curly locks and pale face, she would blend into the leaf angels that she created, for her coat covered her head to toe in a burnt russet red. Their parents eventually catch up to them, laughing as they run, though out of breath. The leafy tapestry crunches beneath their feet as they gather logs, sticks and ivy vines from the surrounding circle to begin building a den. Once the Den is built, the family gather inside it. The children's father produces a handful of sweets from his pocket, and the family munch together, admiring their handiwork. Ben leans into his mother, placing his right hand on her tummy and stroking his thumb back and forth. Their eyes meet, joy finding them once again in the season of change.

Low-slanting sun rays stretch across the forest as the sun begins to hang lower in the sky. The air is cooler now, any warmth from the sun has somewhat vanished from the space. Elsa and Sarah walk hand in hand, chatting about anything and everything, not a hint of awkwardness about them. They wander through the forest and dismantle a den in the clearing for firewood.

Upon returning to their tent on the campsite, Elsa hurries into the tent to grab a grey blanket while Sarah arranges the campfire. After assembling the firewood, she strikes the flint, and the dried leaves in the firepit catch alight. Sparks fly off the flames like little kisses into the ether, and the reflection of the bonfire twinkles in Sarah's eyes. Elsa emerges from the tent holding a packet of biscuits and some marshmallows, as well as the blanket, which she wraps around their backs as they sit facing the fire. The pair huddle close to each other, Sarah's arm round Elsa's back, and they continue chatting while making s'mores and eating them together.

The night draws in, and the light begins to fade. The fire dims: however, the embers refuse to be put out. Sarah and Elsa stand up and hold each other close, slow dancing to the sound of a nocturnal choir. Sarah whispers, "My love for you is like the embers of this fire. It will never burn out". She blows gently into the pit where the roaring fire had been, and together, they watch it catch onto the remaining dried leaves. The fire starts up again as Sarah gets down on one knee, pulling a box from her pocket with a rose gold ring inside.

Autumn sees everything that day, so much love and so much change from the seasons before. As night falls, the forest grows silent, but the promise of old affection, new life and a changing love made her seem wildly alive. She saw a thousand stories come into fruition that year, and she knew she'd see a thousand more in years to come; the seasons bringing about the most natural and authentic love stories that the world would ever see.

Printed in Great Britain
by Amazon